Tye Watkins
In

Tye Watkins-U.S. Marshall

Book Nine of the Tye Watkins series

Gary McMillan

Authors Note

At the start of the Civil War all the federal troops were pulled from the forts in Texas and sent back east. During this time the Apache, Kiowa, and Comanche regained control of the land. They along with the border bandits that were jumping back and forth across the Rio Grande River which separated Texas and Mexico were making life along the Border a very dangerous place to try and raise a family.

Fort Clark, which is located thirty-five miles from the Border near present day Del Rio, was one of the forts abandoned at this time. At various times during the war it was occupied by the Texas mounted Rifles (later know as Texas Rangers) who were a organized outfit made of tough men who tried to stem some of the violence from the border bandits and Indians. At other times the fort was home to troops of the southern army.

After the War federal troops were sent back to Texas. The old forts were again active and several new forts were built to try and protect the influx of homesteaders that were moving into the area. Along the Border the Apache were fighting for what they considered their land and the bandits were taking advantage of the fact there was few lawmen. They stole what they wanted and killed anyone who opposed them.

This was the how it was when Fort Clark was again occupied by the army. Tye Watkins was Chief of Scouts and he and other scouts at other forts along the border and the army together faced the job of trying to rid the land of the bandits and Apache. It was a daunting task and before it was completed hundreds of men, women, and children would lose their lives along with a great number of soldiers and scouts.

Fort Clark, because of its close proximity to the border, had more encounters with the Apache than all the other forts along the border combined during this time.

Tye Watkins

Tye Watkins father, Ben Watkins, was one of the original mountain men who trapped beaver in the Rockies with Jim Bridger and Shakespeare McDovitt from the early 1820's until the beaver craze ended in the mid-thirties. He left the Rockies and headed to a place where he heard there was land for the taking, the new Republic of Texas. He fell in love in San Antonio and married a beautiful lady named Lori. They homesteaded some land near the Rio Grande River and in 1839 had a son they named Tyrone, but would call him Tye.

From the time Tye could walk until Ben was killed by Indians in 1859, young Tye was taught everything he needed to know to survive in this harsh country. Over the years Tye took these things taught to him by his father and became better than his father had been. As a Ranger he tracked down so many outlaws they put a bounty on him, but no one could collect it. When he became a scout for the army he became a target for the Apaches gaining a reputation among them as a great warrior whose death would be a great 'coup' for any warrior. Many had tried over the years.

A month after his encounter with the Apache Yahzie, Tye decided he had enough of fighting Apaches. He had been on their 'most wanted' list for fifteen years and he decided that now, with the responsibility of a family it was time for a change. He had Rebecca write a letter to Governor Edmond Davis to see if the offer made to him a year ago by his predecessor Governor Pease as a Deputy U.S. Marshall was still on the table. He knew he would be gone a lot from home and tracking outlaws would be dangerous, but nothing compared to chasing Apaches. The letter from the governor came two weeks ago with the news that he was elated Tye had accepted the offer and Tye

4

needed to report to the district U.S. Marshall in San Antonio for his appointment. Tye had returned to Clark yesterday with his badge. He was now Tye Watkins, Deputy U.S. Marshall. He would continue to work out of Fort Clark for the time being and would have an area of about 900 square miles he would cover along with a few other deputies.

Shakespeare McDovitt (nicknamed Buff)

Shakespeare was one of the original mountain men who was Ben Watkins best friend in the Rockies during the era of the beaver craze. When the beaver trapping ended he, Jim Bridger, and Ben went their separate ways promising to stay in touch. Ben wrote a letter inviting Buff, who never married, to come live with him and his wife in Texas. Buff started to Texas several times over the next twenty years, but something always came up preventing him from going. He was scouting for the army in Colorado when he heard from soldiers that were transferred up there from Texas about this young scout name Watkins that was making quite a name for himself along the Border. He also had heard about his friend being killed and deeply regretted his not going to see him. The rumor was that this young scout's pa had been a mountain man. Buff decided to go see if the youngster was his old friend's son. He is seventy-one years old now and lives with Tye and his Wife Rebecca on the fort and has spent a lot of time telling Tye stories about his pa.**

Note: read book six "Back to the Rockies**"

Other Books in the Tye Watkins Series

Chapter One

The merchants along Main Street were opening their windows and sweeping off the wooden porches in front of their establishments preparing for another day as the three men rode slowly down the middle of the street. None of the merchants gave these men a second glance as they looked like every other cowboy that rode into San Antonio. Maybe if they had taken a second look they might have seen things different and the disaster that occurred might not have happened.

The three men's clothes were dusty but obviously of better quality than the average working cowboy. Each man's Colt was worn low on his hip, tied down and had seen plenty of use. Each man held the reins loosely in his left hand, his right resting on his thigh close to his Colt. The men's mounts were not working cowboy stock, but rather heavily muscled, built for speed and endurance. If one looked closely at the men's faces, he would see hard faces, faces that had stared down trouble and death many times. Close inspection of these men would tell you that these were dangerous men, men not to tangle with, and men looking for trouble.

The oldest of the three brothers and riding slightly in front was Cole Frazier. Cole was thirty-five years old, Ben was twenty-nine and the youngest, Jud, was twenty-two. Cole and Ben had thick black beards, neatly trimmed while Jud was clean shaven. The two older brothers were six foot tall and thick through the shoulders and muscled arms from years of baling hay, cutting lumber, and pushing a plow in their younger years on the farm in Missouri. Jud was slender and by far the best looking of the three. He fancied himself quite a ladies man and this more than once led him to trouble.

Cole's head never moved, but his eyes moved quickly from left to right and back again looking for anything out of the ordinary. He had left Arkansas three weeks earlier along with his two brothers and the other three men that made up his gang. They had left with the law hot on their heels after robbing three different banks of close to thirty thousand dollars. Seven people had been shot and killed in the robberies and on the last; a little eight year old girl had been trampled to death by their horses.

Dirk Moreland, one of the gang members had scouted the bank in San Antonio for several days while the rest camped a few miles away. He had worked for a survey company a few years ago so he knew the ins and outs of drawing a detailed map. He had drawn a map of the downtown area where the bank was located and notes as to what businesses were close by and the hours they opened. He also had noted the times the town Marshall and his deputies made their rounds. Cole had studied the map carefully and he was surprised how everything he was seeing now was exactly how the map showed it to be. He wasn't a man easily impressed, but he was growing to appreciate the talents of Dirk. He and his brothers rode slowly looking at all the stores and in particular, for any lawmen. Any sign of trouble, anything different from what Dirk had written and drawn, the job would be called off.

The bank they intended to hit was the largest of the banks in San Antonio. The town was growing every day and now totaled upwards to nine thousand people.

Businesses were prosperous and that meant money in the banks. The man who owned the bank was, according to Dirk, very punctual in opening the banks doors at exactly eight o'clock. The marshal and the two deputies on duty drank coffee in the marshal's office every morning and began making their rounds shortly after eight o'clock. The marshal's office was less than a half block from the bank. The plan was for Cole and Ben to enter the bank a minute after it opened. Jud was to be just outside keeping watch and to give covering fire if things went south. Two gang members, James Hayward and Tom Connors, were stationed across the street from the marshal's office and were to make sure the marshal and his deputies could not get out the door if shooting started. Dirk was lounging in a chair two blocks farther down. If things went awry, he would be in position to give covering fire to keep the merchants and townspeople's heads down long enough for the gang to make their way out of town. The sheriff's office was on the street behind the bank and four blocks down. According to Dirk, he didn't get his tail up and moving until well past eight o'clock.

The rest of the plan only concerned the brothers. Cole and his brothers intended to kill the other members after the job and split the money three ways instead of six plus take the men's share they had left from the jobs in Arkansas. From the information Dirk had accumulated, they figured they would split upwards of thirty thousand dollars on this one bank job making a pretty good payday-maybe even retirement on a ranch somewhere after splitting the other money from the jobs in Arkansas from their dead friends.

Cole and his brothers rode with backs straight, shoulders square. All had fought in the war and had been on the losing side. Cole had been wounded in the leg and walked away from the war with a noticeable limp. Ben and Judd had escaped being physically wounded, but both left with a morbid outlook on life and death. Neither had any regards for another man's life-or a woman's either for that matter.

Cole led the gang by being the only one with enough sense to plan things out and to keep them a step ahead of the law. The others idea of pulling a job was to go in, take the money and kill the witnesses and anyone else who got in the way. Cole had no qualms about killing a man, but he didn't kill just for the sake of killing.

As the three men approached the bank, James who had been sitting across the street watching things, walked away to take up his post with Tom in front of the marshal's office. A large, well dressed man with dark pants, white shirt, and bow tie was unlocking the banks door as the three outlaws reined their mounts in front of the bank. The man looked over his shoulder and gave the three men the once over as two more men, probably clerks Cole figured, came from across the street and walked in with the big man. Cole and Ben stepped down from their saddles and handed their reins to Jud and followed the men into the bank pulling their Colts as soon as they were inside. The metallic sound of their Colts cocking caused the three men to turn around.

"Unlock the safe and get the money out and no one will get hurt," Cole said motioning toward the safe with the barrel of his Colt.

The fat man with the bow tie smiled and in a pompous voice said, "Surely you jest my good man. Do you know who the marshal is? Why he will…"

Cole kicked one of the clerks in the groin and when he doubled over he cracked his skull with the barrel of his three pound Colt. "Does it look like we are kidding you son-of-a bitch?" He then hit the fat man in the mouth with his left fist splitting the man's lips and loosening some teeth. "Now open the damn safe." The man, holding his hand over his mouth and blood running between his fingers, hurried to the safe and started turning the combination lock. It didn't open the first time and Cole stuck the barrel of the Colt against the back of the man's head.

"You have one more chance and then you are a dead man." The fat man was whimpering like a baby, sweat rolling off his forehead as he tried once more. This time the safe opened and Cole pushed the man aside and looked in. Money was stacked neatly in huge piles everywhere he looked. More money than he had ever seen before.

"Watch them Ben," he said as he pulled a sack from his belt, holstered his Colt, and started filling it with greenbacks. When the sack would hold no more he pulled his Colt and looked at Ben.

"Let's go," he said and headed toward the door.

"COLE," Ben shouted suddenly and Cole whirled around just in time to see one of the bank clerks pulling a gun from under the counter. Ben's bullet caught the man in the throat. He then shot the fat man.

Almost every man on the frontier at this period of time wore a gun on his hip. When the shots were heard coming from the bank reaction was swift. Shots could be heard outside as Ben and Cole hurried out the door.

Out side Jud was firing his gun and holding the reins of the three horses that were stomping, snorting and causing all kinds of hell. Ben and Cole grabbed their reins from Jud and were doing their best to get mounted as the horses jerked their heads and stomped around in circles with eyes as big as saucers. All three managed to get in the saddle and headed down the street where the others were. They heard shots from the direction they were headed. A couple of merchants fired at them as they rode by, but hit no one. They quickly ducked back into their stores as bullets from the three outlaws splintered the wooded walls around them.

As they raced down the street the two gang members who had been across from the marshal's office jumped into their saddles and joined them, headed out of town at a dead run. Cole did notice three men lying outside the marshal's office. A few more shots were fired in their direction, but covering fire from Dirk drove the merchants back into their stores. Two miles out of town on the Old Mail Road, they slowed their horses to a walk letting them blow.

"That was close," Jud muttered. He looked at Cole, "What the hell happened in the bank?"

"Stupid kid pulled a gun from under the counter and Ben shot him, then he shot the man who opened the safe," Cole answered.

"Why did you kill the banker?" Jud asked.

"Seemed like the thing to do," Ben said as he replaced the spent cartridges in his Colt.

Judd laughed. "Well, you sure stirred up a whole lot of hell."

Each man stepped from the saddle and gave a little water to their mounts then climbed back in the saddle and moved off at an easy gallop.

"Where're we heading?" Dirk questioned.

"West," Cole answered. "To Mexico and all the ladies you can handle."

Sheriff Thompson stood over the bodies of the marshal and the deputies with a grim, determined look on his face. Marshall Lambert had been a good friend of his and a damn good man as well as an outstanding lawmen. He looked at the crowd gathering. "I need fifteen men for a posse. I want men who can ride and can shoot. Meet me at my office in ten minutes. Twenty minutes later the men had been sworn in and were riding out of town following the outlaws.

Chapter Two

Tye sat on the porch of his home holding his three month old son, Ben, while Rebecca was busy feeding Ben's twin sister, Nicole. Tye had returned last night from San Antonio where he had been sworn in as a Deputy United States Marshal. It would be a big change for Tye in a lot of ways. His whole life to this point had consisted of fighting the Apache who for years had him on their 'most wanted list'. He would still be tracking men down, but his quarry now would be men who were outside the law. He knew his new profession would be dangerous, but no way had he figured as dangerous as tracking down Apaches.

While in San Antonio he had visited with other marshals hoping to receive some advice and tips about the job from their experiences, but that didn't pan out as much as he had hoped. It seemed most of the conversations were one sided, his side on fighting Apaches. His reputation had preceded him and the other marshals had a thousand questions about his experiences. Before leaving he had been given a crash course on the law and what he could do and not do as a marshal. He had also been given a leather bound book on the law to read when he could. It was a thick book and Tye knowing he struggled with making out words at a fast pace was elated when Rebecca said she would read it to him when they had time. He also was given a list of men wanted for robbery and a couple for murder and one man that was wanted for about every crime a man could think of. This was the one he would start out with because he figured this man needed to be put away the worse of all.

Jack Gillespie, better known as 'Bloody Jack' was the man's name. He had slain a whore in Fort Worth and killed a man over a poker game in Austin. He had robbed a bank in San Antonio and killed a couple more men and was supposedly now somewhere in the vicinity of Fort Clark.

This was not counting the men he killed in what was supposedly fair fights.

Buff was sitting on the porch with Tye and took Ben from Tye and gently rocked back and forth with the little tyke cradled in his arms. Tye smiled at the scene; a seventy-two year old man who was never around children learning the ins and outs of being a loving grandparent. He was doing a great job too.

Rebecca came out and squeezing between Tye and Buff, sat down on the porch.

"Where's Nicole?" Tye asked.

"She's taking her morning nap." She looked at Buff holding Ben. "Ben needs a nap too, but it looks like he's happy where he is." Buff just smiled and kept rocking.

Tye stood up suddenly. "Trouble may be coming," he said nodding his head toward the path leading to their home. Major Thurston, Fort Clarks Post Commander, was walking briskly toward them. Arriving, he shook Tye's and Buff's hands, removed his hat and bowed to Rebecca.

"You look lovely this morning, Rebecca."

"Why thank you major. A woman can't get enough compliments like that-not around here anyway." She looked at Tye and laughed. "It's nice to have a gentleman around every once in awhile,' she added smiling.

Tye laughed and looked back at Thurston. "Now that you got me in trouble, what do we owe this visit too?

"I know you have," he hesitated for a moment trying to think of the right word, "Retired, but something has come up I need your advice on." He looked up from his friends on the porch and looked away-to the north. "There's a rumor that Quanah Parker is coming down from the northern plains looking for Apache horses and women. He's a bad one and I figure he's going to cause trouble to more than just the Apache."

"Quanah," Tye said, astonishment showing in his tone. "Here along the border?" He sat down and was quiet for a moment then asked. "Who told you?

"Dispatch rider from Fort Stockton came in about an hour ago. Supposedly some friendly Kiowa that lived close to the fort told Major Hennessey, the Post Commander, that they had seen a large party of Comanche headed south led by Parker. The only reason they figured was to raid and steal Apache horses and take women and children for slaves."

Buff, being new to Texas had been quiet, but asked, "Who is this Quanah Parker?"

Thurston answered. "He is a young war chief that has been causing holy hell up north of here. He is the son of a white woman that was taken captive in about '36 on a raid at Fort Parker when she a youngster. She was adopted into the tribe and given the name of Nadua which translates into 'someone found'. A few years later she became the property of Peta Nocona, a great warrior and the son of Chief Iron Jacket."

"You mean he's a breed." Buff blurted out. "Never heard of no breed leading any Indians."

Tye looked at Buff. "This here Quanah is someone special. I think he had to prove every day growing up that he was the equal or better than the other youngsters. This made him more Comanche than the Comanche. Like you mentioned, it would take someone special to lead being half white-and he's that someone. They have pretty well played hell with the settlers and army a hundred and fifty plus miles north of here."

"You mention Quanah's name up there on the plains and the panhandle of Texas and you get an immediate reaction of fear and respect for him from settlers as well as the army,"
Thurston added.

"Were the Kiowa sure it was a war party?" Tye asked.

Thurston nodded. "About two hundred or so warriors traveling light and fast with no women or children."

Rebecca took little Ben from Buff's arms and held him tighly against her breast. "Do you think they will attack the fort here?"

Tye put his arm around her. "No honey, he won't attack the fort. He's too smart for that. He won't attack any towns either. They will hit any homesteads that are in their path or maybe hunting parties they come across such as buffalo hunters. They have a special hate for them."

Rebecca looked at her husband. "Why for buffalo hunters?"

"North of here as far as you can travel in two or more months are great herds of buffalo. These animals are the mainstay of all the plains Indians: The Kiowa, Comanche, Sioux, Cherokee, Cheyenne, Nez Perce and others."

Rebecca smiled at Tye. "And just how do you know all this my dear? You have never been up there."

"Pa talked a lot about the different tribes up in that part of the country for your information Mrs. Smarty Pants," he answered laughing.

"Kno'd all those tribes well," Buff said. "Fought again most of them at one time or nuther.. You left out the most white man hating bunch of all-the damn Blackfeet and the Bloods."

Tye said. "I know pa told me all about them but I thought they were in the mountains mostly."

"The Bloods were, but the damn Blackfeet were on the plains also." Buff said and looked at Rebecca. "You have to understand that the buff has always been the main source of food, clothing, and even shelters for these Injuns. The buffalo hunters come in and kill thousands of the great animals and take only the tongues and hides leaving the rest to rot or be eaten by the scavengers. The Injuns know their way of life is in danger because of these hunters and that is why there is such a hate for them."

Rebecca nodded her understanding. "I feel sorry for them then."

"I always have," Tye said somberly. "They are all like the Apache we have here; fiercely prideful, great warriors, resourceful, and tough as nails. The white race for the most part would starve to death if they had to live the way the Indians do. They have always gone where they wanted to go and live the way their fathers did-free. They now see that life slipping away."

Thurston cleared his throat getting the others attention. "We need to get back to the problem we have-or might have here. Tye, do I send a patrol out to find out or wait till there is a problem. I'm pretty shorthanded now. I keep three or four patrols out all the time and that's about forty to sixty troopers."

"Is Dan scouting for a patrol now?"

"No. He came in yesterday."

Let him lead a small patrol, maybe him and four others, to find out if the rumor is true or not."

"If it is and they are two hundred Comanche- that would be suicide."

"Dan can keep them out of trouble. It would only be a patrol to find out if the rumor is true or not. Give them specific instructions not to engage the Comanche in any way."

Thurston nodded. By the time they return the other patrols will be back. I can hold back on sending out any more since there has been no Apache trouble lately. I would be at full strength if there is a problem with Quanah." He nodded and said. "It's settled then. I'll contact Dan and get things going." He shook Tye's and Buff's hand. "Always a pleasure seeing you Rebecca." He bowed slightly to her, turned and strode swiftly away.

Tye stood up. "I guess I'd better get my things together. I need to get after this Gillespie fellow. He watched Thurston until he passed out of sight. "I sure hope that rumor isn't true." Tye, dressed in his blue cavalry pants, leather boots, a light blue cotton shirt, and his grey campaign hat, sat at the table and re-read the list of names given him to find. Jack Gillespie had a brother that had a ranch about sixty miles north of Fort Clark. He would start his search there. He strapped on his gun belt and checked the Colt to make sure it was clean and loaded. He slipped his Bowie in the top of his right boot and took the Henry from the rack on the wall checking it also. He took his saddlebags from the wall and in one side put some coffee beans, jerky, matches, and a few biscuits Rebecca had made for him. He placed an extra shirt, his moccasin boots and a box of ammunition for his Colt and one for the Henry in the other side. He was ready to leave, but decided to visit with his family for a little while longer. What difference would a day or so make and he wanted to spend a little more time with his wife and babies. He put his guns up for now.

Gary McMillan

Chapter Three

Two hundred and fifty miles northwest of San Antonio a large band of Comanche were preparing to leave their camp on the upper Rio Pecos River. They had been camped there for three days resting up from their raids on settlers on the flat prairie between Fort Stockton and Fort Chadbourn. They would travel south, avoiding patrols from Fort Lancaster along the way in order to reach the area along the border. They were going to kill any settlers who they found, but they were mainly going to raid the hated Apaches, steal their horses and take their women for slaves.

Little Bear, Crooked Nose, and Little Wolf sat on their ponies waiting on their chief to mount his great paint whose rope halter Little Bear held. Soon, they saw him emerge from the mass of warriors who were milling about the camp on their ponies. Six foot tall, broad across the shoulders and deeply muscled with a beautiful headdress of eagle feathers, Chief Quanah Parker strode toward them. Without a word, he took the halter rope from Little Bear and leaped on the paints back. He trotted the pony south, his three close friends following along with over one hundred and fifty warriors. This was a raiding party and there were no small children and no women. There were several boys thirteen and fourteen years old who were along for the experience and to watch the pony herd at night, but would not be involved in any fighting.

The warriors rode light meaning they only carried their weapons, dried buffalo jerky and pemmican for food, and a gourd that held water. There were no cumbersome wagons or pack mules to carry supplies as the stupid soldiers did when they traveled. The Comanche were known to be the best horsemen on the frontier and because of their not being burden with excess baggage could travel fifty or more miles a day easily and eighty if pushed.

Quanah motioned with his hand and three warriors galloped out in front to serve as scouts. One would stay a mile or so in front and the other two off to each side. The raiding party would travel three or four hours before stopping to rest their ponies. They had killed a lone buffalo along with her calf four days ago. They had built racks and dried the meat in strips as well as their women could have done. They distributed the meat, almost five hundred pounds, equally among the men.

Quanah was destined to be one of the greatest of the Comanche chiefs. In later years he would be a great ambassador for his people in the white man's world, but for now, he was leading his people in a fight for their very existence against the white man. Raiding the Apaches and stealing their horses would help in this fight. The taking of Apache women for slaves and raising captive children to be Comanche would help too.

The band traveled at a leisurely pace and had covered about twenty-five miles when Quanah stopped them again to rest the horses. He sat with his trusted friends. A few minutes later one of the scouts came riding in leaped off his pony and quickly walked to where the four warriors sat. Man Who Sees Far was the best tracker in Quanah's band. His named wasn't always Man Who Sees Far, but given to him a few years ago by Chief Iron Jacket because of his remarkable vision.

"I have found a white mans camp with many horses and wagons. I think they hunt tasiwoo (buffalo)."

"How many men?" Quanah asked. The scout held up eight fingers.

"Why do you think they hunt tasiwoo?"

"I have seen the heavy wagons before used by men who kill tasiwoo for their hides. These are same wagons."

Quanah motioned for Man Who Sees Far to sit with them and then spoke. "We can use the horses and if they are as you say, men who hunt tasiwoo, t-

hey will have the guns that shoot far and the heavy bullets for them. These we can use, but we must be careful in our planning the attack. These men, if they are tasiwoo hunters, will be skilled with the gun and we could lose many warriors." The others nodded in agreement.

"What do we do then?" Little Bear asked.

"Where did you see these men?" Quanah asked of Man Who Sees Far.

"Ahead of us, riding toward us. They move slowly because of the wagons."

Quanah sat with his back straight, head up, and now, his eyes closed. His friends knew this sign-he was thinking, planning, scheming, so they sat quietly, waiting.

Quanah sat for a full minute without moving, hardly breathing before speaking. He eyes opened and he began to speak. "We must be sneaky like the fox, quite like the mouse for my plan to work. We will circle around behind them and be like a shadow to the wagons following them, but remaining unseen. When it is dark and they make camp, we will move in close in the darkness. When it is light enough to see we will kill them as they began to move about the camp."

"It will be hard to move quietly with so many of us." Little Wolf said.

"Twenty will be enough if all goes well. The others will wait away from the camp and come in after we attack. We will take only the most experienced warriors to move in the darkness."

The Comanche mounted and followed Man Who Sees Far. Before long they were close enough to see the wagons while lying on their bellies on top of a hill. Quanah agreed with Man Who Sees Far assumption they were hunters of the tasiwoo. All Indians hated these men more, if that was possible, than the average white man because they were taking away their source of life. History would prove that the killing of the buffalo hastened the end of the

Redman's way of life. The main source of their food, clothing, lodging, and even tools came from the buffalo.

"We will ride that way," Quanah said pointing to the west. "They will see our tracks and think we did not see them." The large band rode west leaving a trail even a white man couldn't miss.

"Lookee here!" The bearded man named Luke hollered. He was in front of the wagons and waited for the men who were on horses came up to him. He pointed to the tore up ground. One of the other men dismounted for a closer look.

"Sweet Jesus," Matt Rollins said. "These are Indian pony tracks and a hell of a lot of them."

"Why didn't they attack us?" George asked. George Baker was only twenty and this was his first trip away from home.

Matt looked at him and spit a wad of tobacco juice that hit one of George's boots. "Because they didn't see us stupid. If they had we would be up to our ass in Injuns." George started to bow up to Matt for spitting on his boot, but common sense took over. He was outweighed by fifty pounds and had never been in a real fist fight before. He knew the man was mean as they come and he would probably be in for a lot of pain. He tucked tail and backed down and out here, that was a mistake. The other men lost what little respect they did have for the young man. On the frontier, a man may get whipped every day of the week, but he would have men's respect for not backing down. That's the way it was.

"Ya'll keep the wagons moving north but ride ready for trouble," Matt said. "The Indians are headed west so I'll follow them a ways and make sure they ain't going to circle and come in from behind us." Matt was fifty years old and was an old battle tested veteran of the War. Since then, he had been in several Indian fights including the first one in"64 at Adobe Walls. He knew something about tracking and surviving so the men figured it was a good idea for him to be the one to follow the Indians.

Matt had followed the tracks for about three miles before he began to get that feeling of being watched. He reined in his horse and stood in the stirrups looking in all directions. The land all looked the same-mostly flat with long grass that moved with the breeze making it look like waves on a huge lake. The only sound was the snorting of his horse and his own heart beating. He saw nothing, but the feeling in his gut told him to go back and damn quick.

As he reined his horse around he looked over his shoulder at where he had been headed. A quarter mile away, four Indians had magically appeared. He saw two more to his left and also on his right all about the same distance from him. He nudged his horse into a trot and tried not to look like he felt, scared stiff. He didn't look back but glancing to the right and left, he saw the Indians trotting with him keeping their distance. He continued for another minute then let out a rebel yell kicking his horse into an all out run.

Laying low in the saddle he saw the Indians running their ponies with his and angling in closer. He jerked his Henry out of the leather on the saddle and using the barrel, whipped his horse across the flanks to get more speed.

"OH GOD!" he shouted when he saw the twenty or so Indians in front of him.

His only chance was to make a break to the right or left where only two Indians were-he broke right heading right toward them. He replaced his rifle in the scabbard and pulling his Colt leaned low in the saddle so not to give much to shoot at. At thirty yards he raised and fired knowing that hitting anything from a running horse was improbable. It was one of the luckiest shots he ever made as the nearest brave somersaulted off his pony and hit the ground hard. Matt fired at the second one. He missed, but then he was past the brave and nothing ahead but open prairie. He thought he might have a chance. That chance was short lived.

He heard the shot just as his horse stumbled, slowed and fell. Matt leaping away from the falling horse knew he was dead man for sure. He scrambled to the fallen horse and lay beside it looking over the saddle at the Indians racing toward him. His repeating Henry was in the leather under the horse and useless. He pulled the heavy Sharps from leather on this side of the saddle and lying it across the saddle took sight on the nearest Indian that was maybe two hundred and fifty yards away and coming fast. He squeezed the trigger and the boom of the rifle was deafening. A brave was lifted off his ponies back when the heavy 50 caliber slug hit him and when he hit the ground another warrior went down as his pony stumbled over the rolling body. The Indians split and went to the left and right.

Matt threw the single shot Sharps aside and drew his Colt back out and knocked two more of the red devils from the saddle at forty yards. He started to fire again but he was hit hard in the right shoulder and dropped his Colt. He rolled and picked it up with his left hand, but before he could raise it to fire again something slammed into his chest knocking him on his back. He shut his eyes for a second trying to figure out what happened and when he opened them, he was looking into the eyes of a grinning Comanche. He never felt the club splitting his skull.

Man Who Sees Far looked down on the man he had just killed. A Comanche was no different than an Apache or any other Indian; they respected courage and sometimes did not mutilate their victim who demonstrated it. Man Who Sees Far did not scalp this white man. He picked up the big rifle and the man's Colt. He found some of the heavy cartridges in one of the bags on the man's saddle. He also took Matt's big Bowie out of its sheath. It was a much better knife than the one he had so he pitched his old one to a friend and placed the new one in his beaded leather sheath. A couple of fellow warriors helped him turn the dead horse enough to get the Henry from under him. They picked up the bodies of their dead friends and lay them across their ponies back.

He and the others had ridden for only a couple of minutes when he saw Quanah and the rest of their fellow warriors coming. They held up their ponies and waited. When the two groups met he informed Quanah of what had happened. They moved on following the wagons after burying their friends in shallow caves along the rim of a canyon.

~~

Several miles west of San Antonio, the outlaws had been riding for a little over two hours when Jud, riding a few feet behind Cole and Ben, hollered at his brothers.

"Something's wrong with my horse!" Both men turned in the saddle and looking back at their little brother each could plainly see something was definitely wrong; Jud's horse was favoring his right front leg. Reining in, they all dismounted to take a closer look. Cole raised the front leg and looked at the shoe. It was fine, then looking higher he saw the problem. The horse's fetlock was swollen. He let the hoof fall to the ground and straightened up.

"Fetlock is swollen pretty badly." He looked at Jud. "Your horse is gonna be down for awhile Jud."

"What the hell am I gonna do for a ride?" Jud asked, looking first at Cole and then Ben.

"Posse has some horses," Cole said. "Looks like we're gonna have to get you one of theirs."

"Just how in hell we gonna do that?" Tom asked. "We just gonna go up and ask to borrow one of them." He and the other two members of the gang snickered, but shut up quickly when Cole spoke.

"We're gonna kill every one of the bastards."

Ben looked at his brother like he had lost his mind. "Kill them!" he said, astonishment showing in his voice. "We going to go up against them when they'll probably have us outnumbered at lest two to one and maybe more."

"Look ahead of us at that canyon," Cole said. "If I was a damn Injun, that's where I'd set an ambush." All the men looked at where he was looking. Jud and Ben smiled while the other three just looked and wondered what kind of crazy idiots they were hooked up with. Dirk, James, and Tom had already discussed their plan of leaving these crazy brothers before they got all of them killed. Cole's plan to sit and wait on the damn posse only proved to them the brothers were crazy as a damn loon. They figured the posse would have a minimum of fifteen to twenty men after they killed those men in the bank and the marshal and his men. They would be pissed and in a killing mood too. The three would just have to wait their chance to get away from these crazy bastards.

They rode the quarter mile to the canyon and the closer they got, the better it looked to Cole. Reaching the mouth of the canyon they reined up. After a minute, Cole told them how they would trap the posse. Five minutes later, the horses were hid and the men were in their places. Three were on each side of the canyon spaced twenty yards or so apart. Each understood they would not show themselves until Cole fired his Henry. The men settled in to wait.

Sheriff Thompson sat in the saddle studying the jumble of tracks on the ground trying to figure out what they meant. He was a fair tracker and could read sign better than most. He knew one of the outlaw's horses had developed a noticeable limp and it looked like they had dismounted to take a look at it. Looking ahead he didn't like what he saw. He fought enough Apaches and Comanche to know that the canyon ahead could be a death trap. If the horse was as bad as it looked they may just hole up and try to get one of ours. The tracks were heading straight as an arrow to the canyon and from the look of the terrain on both sides they would lose a lot of time if he attempted to bypass it.

"Get your rifles out as we go into that canyon up ahead and ride loose and ready for trouble," he said turning back to the men. He took his Henry out and jacked a shell in the chamber, turned back in the saddle and nudged his horse with his heels. Several clicks from behind him told him the men were doing the same.

He twisted around in the saddle and spoke to the men again. "When we hit the mouth of the canyon, lay low in the saddle and ride like the devil is chasing you." A minute later they were at the canyon's mouth. "Let's go," he yelled as he slapped his horse's rear with the barrel of the Henry and raced into the canyon hell bent for leather.

Cole cursed under his breath when he saw the posse running full out. *"Damn sheriff is smarter than I figured,"* he mumbled to himself as he sighted in on the sheriff. Swinging the Henry to the right following the sheriff he squeezed off a round. Sheriff Thompson slumped in the saddle and then fell head first off his mount; hit the ground hard and rolled several times. The other outlaws opened up with their repeaters firing as fast as they could lever a shell in the chamber. More posse members bit the dust in the first few seconds.

For some unknown reason the remaining posse members reined up. Cole figured it was because the sheriff was down and they didn't know just what to do. Two or three of the riders fired rounds back at the outlaws, but their horses were excited and jumping every which way making any accuracy impossible. More of the confused men went down under a hail of bullets from both sides of the canyon. Four of the men still in the saddle reined their mounts around and made a dash back from where they come. More bullets were thrown in their direction and only two made it out of the canyon and one of them was barely staying in the saddle. When the smoke and dust cleared, thirteen men and five horses could be seen lying on the ground. Not a single outlaw was hit.

Cole and the rest made their way to the floor of the canyon and made sure each of the men on the ground were dead before gathering up the horses. They rifled through the pockets and vest of the dead men as well as their saddlebags. They found plenty of ammunition for their Henrys and Colts as well as a little cash. In the saddlebags they found food; biscuits, jerky, coffee and some sugar. They were as happy as pigs in a sty now that the posse was no longer a threat, had plenty to eat, and a lot of cash from the bank. Things couldn't be better for the gang. Cole figured to make it better for himself and his brothers.

"Ya'll come on over here and we can divvy up the cash," Cole said loud enough for all to hear. The men gathered around him, his brothers on each side him and the other three grinning members facing him, eager to get their share so they could get away these insane brothers. Cole gave it to them, but it wasn't what they expected. He had his reloaded Henry in his right hand hanging at his side pointing at the ground. He quickly raised the barrel and quicker than you could blink fired three rounds, each striking one of the outlaws square in the brisket and then walked over to them and shot each in the head. He laughed and said "We just upped our share boys." Cole and Ben picked a horse for a spare and threw the saddles off them. Jud picked two and threw his saddle on one. They mounted their horses and headed toward Mexico with Ben whistling the popular southern song, *'I wish I Was in Dixie.'*

~~

Less than an hour of daylight was left when the wagons with the buffalo hunters pulled up to make camp. While the coffee was brewing, young George sat beside Luke.

"Shouldn't Matt have joined up with us by now?"

Luke spit some tobacco juice on the ground. "Figger ole Matt done bought it."

"What do you mean by that?" George asked.

"I mean he's dun found them Injuns and got his self kilt."

"You think so?"

Luke spit again before answering. "If he'd been okay, he'd done been here by now. Damn," he cursed. "Me and him rode the trail for a long time together. He was a good friend and hell on wheels in a fight too." He looked to the west at the sunset. "Matt could never get enough of that view," he said nodding toward it.

George looked. "I can see why. It's sure pretty." He looked back at Luke. "What are we going to do?"

"We're going to get ready for some visitors about sunrise. Maybe we can have a little surprise for them."

"You think they are going to attack?"

"Just as shor as God made little green apples sonny. Yur fixing to have yore first experience with some Redskins-maybe your last," Luke answered smiling.

"Luke, that ain't one bit funny."

"Times like this a feller better have a sense of humor or he just might die from worrying and not have to be kilt by the Injuns." He spit the wad out of his mouth. "Get everyone here."

When everyone had gathered around he spoke up. "I figure Matt ran into them thar Injuns and got himself kilt. I also figure those same Injuns will hit us about dawn. We're in a pretty good spot on top of this knoll with a lot of open area in all directions. With these," he held up his

41

Sharps, "I figure with a little luck and good shooting we can keep those red devils at a distance. We need to forte up before turning in. These wagons with the thick walls will give good protection from the arrows and the Henry's the Injuns will be using so make a little room in each for at least two men. The rest of you scoop out a place in the ground under the wagons. Pile the dirt up around the hole to give you more protection. If they come, it will be just as its getting light enough to see. Be ready and one man in each wagon should stay awake at all times to watch for trouble.

An hour later, Luke figured they were as ready as they were ever going to be. He cursed the fact clouds had moved in a few minutes ago cutting out the light from the moon. He was in a wagon with the youngster George who had the first watch. He was making himself comfortable when George spoke up. He could tell the kid was nervous by his voice.

"Luke, do you think we have a chance to beat them off if they come."

"Yeah, we do kid. A lot depends on how they attack and how many they are and if we can shoot straight. In '64 Matt and a group of men fought off several hundred Injuns at a place called Adobe Wells so yeah, we have a chance if things go right."

"That's a lot of ifs," George mumbled. Luke smiled. He liked this kid even though he was green and knew nothing of shooting buff, Injuns, or much else for that matter.

"George," he said, "You're young and don't know better but there is a one thing you need to learn out here and that a man needs to be respected by other men. You lost what respect the others had for you when you backed down from Matt earlier."

"He would have beaten the hell out of me," George stated.

"He would have for a fact son, but out here it don't matter whether you win or lose a fight; what matters is you don't ever back down from one. Men will respect you for that."

George nodded his head. "I'll remember that. Sorter dumb, but I'll remember." Luke laughed.

Quanah smiled. The Great Spirit must be smiling on us as he watched the clouds move in and the land became so dark he could hardly see the man standing next to him. Earlier he knew they were in trouble when he saw where the white hunters had made camp. There was nothing but open ground all around the hill. Now the cloud cover would allow his warriors to get very close before they attacked at dawn.

He had Little Wolf, Running Bear, Man Who Sees Far, and Crooked Nose beside him. Each of you take warriors and surround the white man's camp then move as close as you can in the darkness, but do not attack until I give the sign." Each of the men left to gather warriors to do as Quanah said. Shortly after midnight, they had the camp surrounded and were within forty yards of the wagons and waited, lying on their bellies in the grass.

Chapter Four

Cole and his two brothers made camp a quarter mile off the Old Mail Road. In this part of the country it was never a good idea to camp where anyone riding the road could see you even if you were the outlaw. It was an unwritten law in this part of Texas that you were better off most of the time if no one knew you were around.

Jud, drinking a cup of coffee, laughed suddenly. "I bet those son-of-a-bitches in San Antonio don't forget us for a long time. How many of their up stand citizens did we kill today anyway?"

Ben, always laid back and talked slower than most, answered. "Well, to tell you the truth, I wasn't exactly counting, but it was more than a few."

"Eighteen," Cole spit out. "Eighteen at least. We may have killed more if some of the wounded died." He threw what remained of his coffee on the ground. "You're right though Jud; they ain't likely to forget this day for a long time.

"How'd you come up with eighteen?" Jud asked.

"Marshall and two deputies, two men at the bank, and thirteen at the ambush."

Ben, not as quick witted as his brothers was silently counting what Cole said. "You're right-eighteen." He reared his head back and laughed. "That's a new record for us. Damn!"

Jud slapped his brother on the shoulder. "That ain't counting Dirk, James, and Tom that Cole shot."

"Let's see now; eighteen plus Tom. Dirk, and James-hell, that's twenty-one damn people we sent to their maker today." Ben hooted and slapped his leg. "That's got to be a record for all time."

Jud looked at Cole who wasn't laughing. "How much money did we get Cole?"

"Been thinking about that," Cole said. "While you boys were making a fire and coffee I made a quick count and figure with what we took from the posse, the bank, and our three friends I'd say twenty-five thousand-maybe a little more.

Ben's jaw dropped. "Twen…Twenty-five thousand…dollars," he stammered out unable to believe they had that much.

"Maybe more, maybe a little less" Cole said. "We'll count it when we get to Mexico. We'll be going though a couple towns, Uvalde and place called Brackett. They both have a fort which means lots of soldiers. That means you; me included, had better be on our best behavior and not arouse anyone's attention to us. Understood?" Both brothers nodded their understanding.. "It's late, let's get some sleep."

~~

The small patrol had left Fort Clark at mid morning led by a young lieutenant by the name of James Farley. He was new to this part of Texas, but was by no means a greenhorn that knew nothing about fighting Indians. He had come to Clark from Fort Belknap which was located on the eastern edge of Comanche Territory and about two hundred plus miles northeast of Fort Clark. He had been in several skirmishes with the 'terror of the Plains' as the Comanche were known.

Dan was scouting for the patrol and for the first time Lieutenant Farley. It did not take him long to figure out this was no snotty-nosed sonofabitch smart-ass from the Point, but rather a level headed officer who had been around. Tye would say the lieutenant has been up the river and around the bend. Dan felt comfortable with Farley leading the small patrol.

It was almost dark when they made camp. The small fire for coffee was put out before full dark. Two men would stand two hour watches at all times and the lieutenant would be in the last pair. This impressed the men as well as Dan since officers usually didn't stand guard.

The men sat on their bedrolls, finishing their cup of coffee before turning in. Lieutenant Farley stated that he was sorry he did not get a chance to go on patrol with Tye then quickly added that he no way intended that remark as detrimental to Dan.

Dan chuckled. "No offense taken lieutenant. Every officer should have that experience at least once."

"I understand he knew more about the Apache than the Apache knows about themselves."

Dan nodded. "That could be true. He's thirty now and has been fighting them since he was fourteen and the last five or so years, he has been targeted by them. It would make an Apache big medicine to his people if killed the scout."

"How do you think he will do as a lawmen?"

"I'd say any outlaw that has Tye on their trail is in for a rough time. There is no way once that man has the scent will he lose their trail. He is the best I have ever seen at tracking and reading sign."

"Any of you men been on patrol with Tye scouting?" Farley asked. All of them nodded.

A private Lancaster spoke up. "I was with him three months ago at the fight with Tanza at the place known as the Canyon of the Dead by the Apache. We would have been wiped out, massacred if it hadn't been for him. The last attack by the Apache was something I hope to never see again. We were overrun with Apaches in the arroyo where we were and it was hand to hand fighting with guns, war clubs, knives, sabers, and fist. We were done and we knew it. If you have ever fought an Apache hand to hand- well the average soldier ain't prepared for that. Like I said we were done, but that's when Tye stepped in. He came down the arroyo swinging a Sharps by the barrel and smashing Injuns right and left sorter like Samson did in the Bible with the jaw of an ass. He was screaming louder than the Apache were and it startled them to see this crazy white man among them bashing them right and left. They lit a shuck out of there as fast as they could go. It was something if I live to be a hundred I will never forget." He shook his head and his voice cracked. "Me and every man there owe our lives to that crazy sonofabitch. He's a wonder and I'll always be in his debt. As far as what you asked Dan a few minutes ago, I would say that this part of Texas ain't gonna be so criminal infested after Tye goes to work." He laughed and added. "I wouldn't be in one of their shoes for ten thousand dollars."

They finished their coffee and lay down on their bedrolls, each lost in their own thoughts. An owl swooped low over them looking for a meal and a lonely coyote let his presence be known from a nearby hill. A sentry was posted and soon all was quiet except for a couple of men snoring, the occasional snorting of a horse, and the footfalls of the sentry walking around the camp.

Chapter Five

The eastern sky was just turning grey with the coming dawn when Quanah shot one of the hunters who had walked from behind one of the wagons to relieve himself. A second later all hell broke loose. Warriors appeared to rise magically from the ground only a few yards from the wagons, some firing their repeaters and others loosen arrows at the surprised hunters and teamsters. The roar of the Sharps was deafening as the hunters returned fire and their heavy slugs took a toll on the warriors just as Quanah knew they would, but the chief knew something else; it took time to reload the single shot guns and his warriors would be on them before they could.

That was exactly the case and Luke knew all was lost. "Use your pistols boys," he screamed, but his voice was drowned out by the screaming Comanche that were already on them, jumping in the wagons and slashing the men with knives and tomahawks. Others were dragging the screaming white men out from under the wagons.

Luke shot two with his pistol before taking a stunning blow in the shoulder from a tomahawk that rendered his gun hand useless. He pulled his Bowie with his left hand intending to kill one or more before he bought it, but an eight foot spear struck him in the chest and protruded a foot out his back. He toppled over backwards from the wagon, dead before he hit the ground.

George smashed a brave's face in with the butt of his heavy Sharps then took an arrow in the left shoulder. He staggered back, almost falling out of the wagon. He pulled his pistol and killed another warrior as the man raised himself up over the rim of the wagon to get at him. Someone grabbed the back of his coat and jerked him out of the wagon. He hit hard on his back and instantly a Comanche was standing over him with his knife. George raised his pistol and pulled the trigger. The bullet, traveling upwards struck the Comanche in the groin and continued upwards into his guts. Screaming, the warrior fell away from George who quickly scrambled under the wagon. He saw his friend Luke, lying with the spear in his chest, eyes wide open. "God" he hollered and shot another Indian that was trying to get under the wagon with him. Suddenly he felt hands on his legs and he was being pulled out from under the wagon. As he came out he kicked himself free, rolled over and shot another with his last bullet. He jumped to his feet screaming at the top of his lungs. He was surrounded by six or seven painted warriors who were staying away from this crazy white kid. George had pulled his knife and was twisting and turning, slashing at anything that moved. The warriors were laughing while staying away from the slashing knife. They were going to have a good time with this youngster.

Quanah rode up on his magnificent paint and quickly saw what was going on. He also saw the wagon the boy had been in and noticed the dead warriors all around it. At the same time George fell to his knees exhausted, but he still held the knife. A warrior behind him raised his spear but halted his throwing motion on a sharp command from Quanah.

Quanah dismounted and walked into the circle. The chief spoke fairly good English having been taught by his mother. The boy looked up at him and slowly stood up and faced him. His knife held out in front. Quanah noted the useless left arm, the broken shaft of an arrow still protruding from it.

He stepped back quickly, easily avoiding a slashing knife from George.

George was dumfounded when Quanah spoke. "Put down the knife. We are not going to kill you." He spread his arms. "Enough have died already." George stood there, not believing what he just heard. The Indian spoke again. "Drop your knife. We will not harm you."

Something inside George told him this Indians was a special Indian. Also, Luke or someone told him once that an Indian never lied. He looked at the other faces of the warriors around him and saw nothing but hate in their eyes so he hesitated. He also realized it was real quite so all of his friends must be dead. "Why am I still alive?" he mumbled to himself, but loud enough for Quanah to hear.

"I am Quanah Parker, chief of the Nocona Comanche. I wish to speak with you and then you will be sent on your way."

"Well I'll be," George said. "You're Parker?" He looked hard at the Comanche and noticed his skin was a little lighter than the others and his eyes were not black. He also knew he was a dead man if he fought anymore. He had been told what terrible pain the Redman could inflict on captured men, but for some reason and God only knows why, he trusted this Comanche. He threw the knife, sticking it into the ground. His arms were grabbed from behind and he was quickly tied up. He figured he had made a mistake as he was tied to one of the heavy wagon wheels. He watched as an argument was apparently going on among the Comanche. He knew he was the topic. It lasted for a couple of minutes and then got real quite as he watched the man who called himself Quanah Parker come over and squatted in front of him.

"You're a brave man, not coward like most white men," the Comanche said. He looked over at his warriors. "They want to kill you." He hesitated before continuing and George looked over at the rest of the men and swallowed the lump in his throat. He could imagine being scalped alive, or roasted while tied to this wheel or a hundred other vile things he had heard the Indians do. "I not kill you white man. They not kill you."

"Why?"

"You kill tasiwoo."

"Kill what?" George asked not understanding the word.

"Tasiwoo, you kill buffalo?"

"Never have. This was my first hunt. Looks like it will be my last."

Quanah smiled and stood up pulling his knife and stepped toward George. The lad braced himself for the inevitable that he knew was coming. He was shocked when Quanah slashed the roped that held his hands and then the ones holding him to the wagon. Quanah said something in Comanche to the others and two came over and picked George up. He was surprised they did so gently, like they didn't want to hurt him.

"Sit here," Quanah said pointed to a blanket on the ground. One of the fires from the night before had been rekindled and George could see the flames flaring up. George's knife was stuck in the flames, held there by a grinning Comanche.

I knew it, George thought to himself. *Here it comes. Well, they ain't going to get no pleasure from watching me scream like a woman.* Brought up in a God fearing home he mumbled, *Yeah though I walk through the valley of death I will fear no evil for Thou are with me.* That's all he could remember except something about still waters. He wished he had paid more attention to his mom's Bible reading but it was too late now. The grinning Comanche with the crooked nose was walking to him. *Go ahead and do your worse you savages but you will get no joy from watching this white boy die.* He braced himself and clamped his lips tight. He felt a terrible pain in his left shoulder. He looked down and the shaft was gone. Quanah laid it in front of him on the ground.

A grinning Quanah squatted in front of him. "You might want to keep," he said pointing to the arrow. He pointed to the warrior with the crooked nose who held a glowing red knife. "We have to do this to stop the blood. It will hurt," he said and stuck a piece of rawhide in his mouth. "Bite down hard."

The next few seconds would be the most painful of George's life as the warrior with the crooked nose stuck the glowing blade to the wound in front and back, melting the flesh and sealing up the holes and appeared to be enjoying every second of it. George's face turned red and his eyes bulged some but he didn't pass out and didn't utter a word. This impressed all the warriors.

He was given some water and feeling better, was allowed to stand up. He looked Quanah in the eye. "Why did you let me live?"

"I saw you in battle and you much brave and fought hard."

"I was scared to death."

Quanah laughed. "Maybe so, but you brave-and you are young. Maybe you can help the Comanche."

"Help?" George said, not understanding what he meant. "How can I help the Comanche?"

"By understanding us and telling other white men that we are not the savages they make us out to be. We kill because you, the white man, thinks all this land," he swept his arms around in a full circle, "is theirs. They want it all and we, even though we have been here a long, long time need to get off this land. They kill the tasiwoo for the hides and leave everything else to rot and for the scavengers to feed on. We depend on the tasiwoo for our very existence. It is our food, our clothing, our homes, our tools; it is everything to my people. There is much land, enough for all if you, the white man, would be willing to share. We could live together without killing. Take this to your white brothers and tell them this."

I will," George said. "This I promise you." Quanah nodded and grunted something in Comanche and a horse with a saddle on it was brought to George. The Comanche with the crooked nose handed him his knife. Quanah handed him his Colt and a Sharps with a handful of cartridges.

"Go. Tell them that we are not the savages they make us out to be." George nodded and stepped into the saddle. The Comanche's standing around parted and let him through. He rode a few yards and reined his mount around. He nodded to Quanah, turned his horse and rode off still wondering why in God's name he was still alive when every other man with him was dead. He was sure of one thing though. He would do as Quanah asked and he sure as hell would hunt no more tasiwoo. He would later learn that he was the only white man captured by Quanah who ever lived to tell about it.

~~

Dan and the patrol were traveling north looking for sign of Indians. Dan, as usual was a quarter mile in front, his eyes ever alert, always sweeping the terrain in the direction he was traveling as well as both sides for trouble. His eyes also searched the ground for tracks. A light rain, possibly yesterday, washed most of whatever tracks there were away, but any new ones would be plain to see. Plus he didn't figure the rain was hard enough to wash away the tracks of over a hundred Indian ponies if the report was true.

They were about fifty miles north of Fort Clark when they turned a little west angling toward Eagles Nest.

Dan knew if the Comanche wanted captives they would head for the border and he should cut their trail somewhere before reaching it. He reined his mount to a halt as an Indian appeared a hundred yards in front of him. He could tell it was an Apache and wondered why the brave just sat on his pony, watching him. Dan looked in all directions but saw nothing and the land here was pretty flat except for the small rise in front that the Apache just came from behind.

As he watched, the Apache approached him slowly, his hands held away from his sides. Dan slipped his Henry back into the saddle leather and watched. He recognized the Apache when he was fifty yards away. He nudged his horse forward to meet with Yahzie. They reined in beside each other and each nodded his head to the other.

"It is good to see Tye's friend again."Dan said smiling.

"It is good to see you-Watkins's friend also," Yahzie answered.

"I thought you promised Tye you would not come back into Texas. What are you doing out here.?"

"Word among my people is the Comanche come to kill and take captives. I came to see if this be true or not. I not look for trouble with white man."

"That is why I am here also," Dan said. "We also heard this."

"You come to kill Comanche?"

"Only if we have to." Dan looked to the north. "I have been sent to see if this is true or not."

The small patrol was coming up to them. "Not many men," Yahzie chuckled noting the number of soldiers.

"If we find sign of the Comanche, I will send for many soldiers."

"I ride with you, help you look for sign-yes."

Dan smiled. "Glad to have you along." He turned as the patrol rode up.

Second Lieutenant James Farley had a shocked look on his face as he realized Dan was talking to an Apache.

Lieutenant Farley, I want you to meet my and Tye's friend Yahzie." The Lieutenant, knowing Apaches don't shake hands, tipped his hat.

"Did you say Yahzie?" Farley asked now remembering the name of the Apache that killed several people a few months ago.

"Yes. The same one you are thinking about. He will be riding with us for awhile and I want you and the men to show him the respect an Apache warrior of his stature deserves."

"Ridin…"

"Yes Lieutenant," Dan said cutting Farley off. " Riding with us. He's as curious as we are about the report of Comanche coming down here. That's why he's out here. The word spread among the Apache too."

"Then it's probably true don't you think?" Farley queried.

"I would pretty much bet on it. It might be a good idea to send a rider back to Clark. Thurston may want to get a large force to meet up with us."

Lieutenant Farley took a pad and pencil from his shirt pocket and begins writing.

To Major James Thurston

Post commander

Fort Clark Texas

Sir: We came across the Apache Yahzie who is also looking for the Comanche. Word has circulated among the Apache also of a large party coming to kill and take captives. Our scout, Dan, feels the report is probably true and thought you might want to assemble a column together to meet up with us just in case. If we verify the report is true I will dispatch a rider to meet your column at the

junction of the Rio Pecos and the Rio Grande Rivers to
lead you to where we are.
Your obedient servant
Second Lieutenant James Farley

He handed the dispatch to Dan to read. Dan smiled. "Don't read none too good, Lieutenant." He handed it back to Farley.

Farley nodded and smiled then turned to Sergeant Arnold. "Find a man who knows the way back to the fort and have him give this to Thurston."

"Yes sir," Arnold said flashing a quick salute as he reined his mount around.

"We'll be out in front, Sir," Dan said as he turned and galloped northwest with Yahzie riding beside him.

He watched Dan and the Apache ride off knowing there wasn't a word in the manuals he had read about an Apache scouting for the Army. He shrugged then smiled. He felt fortunate that he had Dan scouting for him on his first patrol into to hostile country. He had hoped it would be Tye, but that wish went up in smoke with Tye becoming a U.S. Marshall. He had heard all the stories about the man, some which were hard to believe.

Farley's father had been a career soldier and had retired after being wounded in the battle at Gettysburg. He had been a major in the Union army. Soldiering was the only thing that James Farley had ever wanted to do. His father, who had a reputation of being an officer who led by example had been extremely popular with his men. Young James had promised himself he would be the same, never asking his men to do something he wouldn't do himself. In battle he would be at the front, not the rear.

Captain McClellan had taken him aside several times and had given some good advice on what he needed to do to have the respect of the men he led. The captain used his own experience as holding himself above the men he led, not listening to anyone .and going strictly by the army manual. The men hated him and had no respect for him. His arrogance had nearly got himself and his men killed and would have if Tye hadn't pulled his butt out of the fire. That day had changed his attitude and demeanor not to mention his career. Since then, with Tye's help, he had the men's respect and they quit looking for reasons to not be part of any patrol he led. It was a good feeling and he hoped the lieutenant would get that feeling some day.

Major Thurston, Captain McClellan, First Sergeant Arnold, and every other officer and non-com he spoke with told him the same thing; listen to Tye or his scouts when you are on patrol and make your decision after that. He promised himself he would. He glanced over his shoulder at the men riding behind him, looked up at the Flag flapping in the breeze and felt a sense of pride in what he was doing.

It was late in the afternoon when Dan and Yahzie saw the horse a quarter mile ahead of them. Dan took out his field glasses for a closer look. The horse was saddled and had his head down munching the short grass. Looking past the horse he could see what looked like a man lying on the ground. Sweeping the glasses right and left, he saw no other horses or men. He replaced the glasses in his saddle bag and nudged his horse forward at a walk. Both men kept a weary eye for trouble. At a hundred yards out the horse raised his head and looked in their direction. Dan figured he must have snorted or nickered because the man on the ground raised himself up. He watched the man look around and then spotting him and Yahzie, picked up his rifle.

At fifty yards, Dan halted and shouted. "I'm Dan August, army scout on patrol from Fort Clark." The man stood with his rifle pointed in their direction but not right at them.

"What do you want?" he hollered back.

"We're on patrol checking out the rumors about a large band of Comanche led by Quanah Parker being around. Thought maybe you had seen something."

If George's shoulder didn't hurt so much he would have laughed. He had seen something okay. He lowered the gun. "Come on in."

Dan and his friend nudged their horses forward and dismounted when they reached the man's horse. The first thing Dan noticed was the man looked more like a kid than a man. The second thing he saw was the arm bandaged and that the youngster was favoring it considerable when he moved.

Dan looked at the man's shoulder and nodded. "Looks like you have a problem. What happened?"

"Those Comanche you asked about?"

"They did this to you?"

George sat down easy, but still grimaced when a wave of pain shot through his shoulder. "I was with a group of buffalo hunters when we were attacked by two or three hundred Comanche. "

"Two or three hundred?"

"Well it seemed to be that many. They were everywhere screaming and shooting arrows and bullets at us. Killed every one of my friends."

Dan kneeled in front of the youngster. "How did you escape?"

"Well, I was in a wagon and shot several of them then I got knocked out of the wagon when the arrow hit me. I lost my rifle and came up swinging my knife and hollering like a mad man. They were in a circle around me when I realized I was the only one making any noise. All my friends were dead. I made up my mind I wasn't going to be captured alive so I kept turning in a circle swinging the knife till I just plum gave out. I was waiting for them to kill me and one was about to, but a shout from another stopped him."

"He stopped?"

"Yes sir. The man who stopped him said his name was Quanah Parker. He spoke good English too."

Dan looked at Yahzie and saw the man stiffen when he heard the only word he had understood-Quanah Parker. Dan looked back at the boy. "Why did he stop them?"

"He said he saw me during the fight and that I fought well to be so young. I told him I didn't know about that, but I was just plum scared to death. He smiled and said it was okay to be afraid sometimes. He took the shaft out of my arm and then a brave took a hot blade and sealed it. We talked for awhile and he told me I was to tell everyone that the Comanche was not the savages they think we are. They are just fighting for their home which the white man claims is his. He said the white man claims everything is theirs. He said they will kill all men who hunt the buffalo though. He said the buffalo was their lifeblood."

"Where did all this take place?"

"I dunno. Back there," he said pointing where he had come from about twenty or so miles. Can't rightly say cause I'm lost as can be. I was just riding in what I figured was south or southwest."

Dan stood up and turned to Yahzie and told him in Spanish what the boy said. The Apache nodded and jumping on his pony headed toward the border.

Dan turned back to George. "Didn't catch your name son?" He extended his hand.

"George Baker," he said shaking Dan's hand.

George started to say something but a racket behind him stopped him. He turned and saw the patrol coming a quarter mile away. "Make a lot of racket to be so few don't they?"

Dan laughed. "And then they wonder why they can never surprise the Indians. Let me help you on your horse and we'll get you back to Fort Clark and get you some doctoring.

The patrol rode up and Dan made the introductions to Farley and Sergeant Arnold. He told them what happened and that the story was true about the Comanche. He recommended they send a man back to Clark with the wounded youngster and advise Thurston of the situation.

"We will follow the tracks of George's horse back to where the fight took place and pick up the trail of the Comanche.

When we figure out where they are headed we can send a man to where the Rio Pecos and the Rio Grande Rivers meet and wait on the column.

"Do you have a man in particular in mind?"

"I would send Sergeant Arnold back. He knows this country as well as me. He can lead the column to us."

Farley nodded and turned in the saddle. "Sergeant Arnold!"

Two seconds later Arnold was at their side. "Yes Sir."

"Scout Dan says you know this country well."

"Yes sir. Been on maybe ten patrols or more up here in the last two years."

"You can find the junction of the Pecos and Rio Grande?"

Arnold turned his head and spit a stream of tobacco that splashed on a flat rock slightly perturbed that the lieutenant would ask him that. "I can find it Sir."

"As soon as we determine where the Comanche are headed you will head there and wait on the column and then bring them to us.

Chapter Six

The Frazier's rode slowly into the town of Uvalde not wanting to attract any attention. They reined in at the first saloon they came to and leaving their horses at the hitching rail, Cole took the saddlebags with the money and walked in. Even though it wasn't noon the place was fairly crowded. They found an empty table and sat down.

"Remember," Cole whispered, "We don't do anything to attract any attention to us." Ben and Jud nodded.

"Pretty busy place to be this time of day," Ben said looking around.

"That must be the sheriff and a deputy standing at the bar," Cole said looking at the mirror behind the bar with the reflection of the two men with their badges on their vest. Knowing Jud had a quick temper and an eye for the ladies he reminded his little brother again to be careful in what he said and did.

"Do you think I'm stupid or what?" Jud replied in a tone that was a little too loud and a couple of men looked their way. The three of them saw this and Jud knew he had screwed up.

Cole's face turned ugly as spoke in a soft, but threatening voice. "That's exactly what I'm damn well talking about you smart-ass little brat. You just don't have any damn sense sometimes. Now sit there, drink your beer and don't open your loud mouth again."

"Hell, Cole. Here comes the sheriff," Ben said. If looks could kill, Jud would be dead three times over when Cole looked at him. Jud dropped his head and stared at his beer. "Let me do the talking," Cole whispered.

"Howdy boys," the man with the sheriff's badge said as he walked up to their table. The sheriff knew all the locals and these were strangers. He had been around for awhile and he knew hard cases when he saw one and the three men had that look.. He had unhooked the strap on his holster that held his gun. "Saw ya'll when you came in. You passing through Uvalde or looking for work."

"Passing through," Cole said. As he spoke, Cole noticed the deputy had his back to the bar and his right hand close to the butt of his Colt.

"Where you headed?"

"West. Thought we might go to Mexico and chase some senoritas," Cole answered becoming a little agitated at the questions. "You always question strangers this way?"

"Nope, not always, but I do when three men ride in together that look the way you do. This is a quiet little town and don't need any trouble."

"Just how do we look?"

"Like men who know trouble. Men who wear their guns tied low and look like they know how to use them. Add the fact that you brought in your saddle bags only raised my curiosity more."

"We're having a drink and then leaving sheriff," Cole said with a smile. "If that's alright with you of course."

The sheriff backed away from the table, his hand now resting on the butt of his Colt. Everyone in the place eyes were focused on the sheriff and the men at the table.

"That's fine, but before you go I'm curious as to what's in those bags. So if you will just empty them on the table and let me take a look you can be on your way"

"Why the interest in our saddlebags?"

"Had a wire a couple days ago about six men who robbed a bank in San Antonio and were headed this way."

"There's only three of us."

"I can see that, but I got another wire that these men ambushed and killed the posse that was after them and three of the outlaws were killed in the fight."

Cole hesitated for a second or two before speaking. "Whatever you say sheriff. Jud, let the sheriff look inside those bags." Jud handed the bags to the sheriff. As the sheriff reached for them, Ben who had his gun pulled and hid under the table pulled the trigger. The bullet went through the table top and hit the sheriff in the chest. At the same time, Cole pulled his gun and shot the deputy in the throat just as the man was going for his gun. The deputy grabbed his throat with both hands and dropped to his knees. Cole shot him again in the chest and quickly turned his gun on the other men in the saloon. "Anyone moves-he dies." He said loudly. Jud picked up the bags and then both he and Ben had their guns on the men also. They made their way quickly to the door holding their guns on the patrons as they moved to the door.

"Crowd gathering," Ben said glancing outside over the bat-winged doors of the saloon.

"Then scatter them," Cole said. Ben fired two quick shot in the air and men were ducking for cover as the three outlaws mounted their horses and rode hell bent for leather out of town. No shots were fired in their direction as no one outside the saloon knew what was going on inside.

"So much for not raising any attention our way," Ben said as they reined in their mounts to a trot.

"That stinking nosey bastard of a sheriff got what he deserved," Jud said.

"He was probably a damn good man," Cole said. "He was just doing his job of trying to keep trouble out of his town. That was stupid on my part of bringing in those bags. That's what got his attention because it's not natural for a cowboy to do that. A cowboy goes in a bar with one of three things on his mind-drinking, poker, or a woman and he don't need his saddlebags to do any of them." He looked back over his shoulder expecting to see the dust of a posse. Seeing none, he nudged his horse into an easy gallop with his brothers following. Cole noticed the telegraph poles were up along the road, but no line was on them yet.

Uvalde was the end of the line at least for now. He was thankful for that.

Back in Uvalde, Major Hamilton, Post Commander of Fort Inge, had Lieutenant James Mason leading a troop of fifteen troopers he had assembled to pursue the outlaws. The lieutenant's orders were to pursue them till they were captured or killed. Lieutenant Mason was sure they would go through Brackett where Fort Clark was located. He was hopeful of seeing his friend, Tye Watkins again.

Mason was a striking figure when one looked at him in his uniform. He was well proportioned body wise and the ladies loved his blue eyes and blonde hair. His hair use to fall to his shoulders until Tye casually mentioned one day that his blonde hair would make a hell of a decoration on some Apache's lance. He had worn it short since. He had met Tye by chance when he was first assigned to Fort Inge and was in San Antonio on his way to the fort. Tye happened to be in San Antonio on his honeymoon at the same time. When the coach left the city toward Fort Inge and Fort Clark, they both were passengers along with Tye's wife who happened to be the most beautiful woman he had ever laid eyes on.

Mason would get off at Inge and Tye going on to Clark. Mason had built a pretty good reputation at Inge and was popular with the troops. He would always give credit to Tye for it because of the things Tye explained to him on the trip in the coach: things like what to expect from the land out here and the cold reception he would get from the 'old veterans' who hated young lieutenant's fresh from the east. He explained to Mason what it would take to earn the 'old guys' respect. He explained he would usually have a scout or two on his patrols, but he needed to learn the lay of the land, the landmarks and where the water holes were so he could lead his men if something happened to the scouts. Last, but not least, before making a decision in the field, listen to the men who had been our there and then go with your gut. Throw away the army manual because it wasn't worth a damn when you are facing a band of screaming Apaches that are intent on killing you. He smiled when he thought of what Tye said each time they saw one another. *Well, Lieutenant, I see some Apache buck still hasn't got that mop of blonde hair. Still say it would make a nice trophy,* and then he would laugh.

They were riding on the Old Mail Road which if a man stayed on it would go all the way to San Diego, California. Due to the traffic on the road there was no way his scout could stay with the tracks of the outlaws so he had two men riding on each side of the road making sure there were no tracks leading away from it. He looked up at the wireless telegraph poles and thought it would have been nice to simply wire Clark about the men heading their way. But then he would not have the opportunity to see his old friend again.

Chapter Seven

Dan and the soldiers with him stood beside their horses. All around them lay the mutilated bodies of the buffalo hunters. Some were in the open and others lay under the burned wagons. It was a sickening sight and one of the troopers, Private Jansen, had already lost what was on his stomach.

"We need to bury them the best we can," Dan said to Lieutenant Farley. I know this ground ain't fit for digging but maybe we can scratch out shallow holes and then cover them with enough rocks to keep the scavengers away." *These men ain't the only ones we're gonna bury before this is over,* he figured.

The lieutenant, though half sick to his stomach also, began barking orders. Two shovels were found that had not burned and two men were digging the best they could while others gathered rocks. In less than two hours the men were buried and Dan and his men were on the trail of the Comanche. It wasn't a hard trail to follow. Tracks of a hundred and fifty or so horses left a trail a blind man could follow and then there was the smoke. Smoke from burned out homesteads were along the trail along with more bodies to bury. Dead children were found which told Dan one thing-this was a war party and they were taking no prisoners that would slow them down. They were here for one thing, killing Apaches and taking their women and horses. Any white or Mexican that was in their path was just those peoples bad luck.

I hope Yahzie got to his people and had time to rally them together before the Comanche crossed the Rio Grande, Dan mused. *They are covering a lot of ground in a hurry, and if he didn't, this is gonna be a bad time for the Apache,* he figured as he looked at the day old tracks.

"You say something?" Carter asked.

"Nah, just thinking out loud sergeant." Dan nudged his horse and the little patrol headed out with every man hoping and praying they didn't stumble by accident into over one hundred damn angry Comanche.

When riding in wild country like this a man had better notice things like bent grass, broken twigs or turned over rocks if he wants to keep his hair. Dan notices all these things without thinking about them-it was just second nature and was the reason he was still healthy. He had learned a lot from Tye the last two years. Things like animals may build their nest or lairs, but they do little to disturb the surrounding countryside. Only man leaves his mark and when one sees something out of place, you can bet it was a man that did it. This was something Tye's pa had preached to Tye over the years. He said the only animal he knew of that altered nature was the beaver when he built his dams in the streams and there ain't any beaver around here.

Dan followed the trail up the slopes to the crest of hills and down the other side. Through the junipers, around mesquite and cactus he rode never veering from the Comanche's trail.

It was late evening when he smelled that familiar smell. He reined his horse in and waited on the other men.

"What is it Dan? What did you see?" Farley asked when the patrol arrived.

"Don't see anything, lieutenant."

Farley looked quickly around sorter confused why they stopped when Dan had been saying they need to hurry all day. "What are we stopping for?"

Dan stood up in the stirrups to stretch his legs some then settled his butt in the saddle, resting his palms on the pommel of his saddle. "Take a whiff of the air and tell me what you smell"

Lieutenant Farley stuck his nose in the air and took a deep whiff. "Woodsmoke-campfire."

"Wood smoke okay, but it ain't no campfire sir."

"What is it then?"

"Homestead and burnt flesh."

Farley took another whiff. "You're right. It does have a different smell to it."

"Tell the men to get ready for another unpleasant sight," Dan said reining his horse back toward the trail and what he was sure would be more dead settlers.

Farley turned in the saddle and gave the news to the men as Dan rode off. He looked at Dan's back and shook his head. The smell of smoke was faint; he probably would never have noticed it. *How in heavens name did he smell it while trotting his horse and reading sign?* He shook his head. "Let's try and stay up with our scout," he said kneeing his horse into a canter.

Dan was about forty yards from the smoldering homestead waiting on the patrol. He could see a woman lying just in front of what was left of the porch. She had several arrows in her and had been scalped, but was still clothed. *They're in quite a hurry not to take the time to rape and torture her.* A daughter that looked about seven or eighty years old lay beside her, a single arrow in her back. *They didn't even take the time to remove their arrows,* he noticed. The man of the house wasn't scalped or mutilated, a sign of respect by the Indian. He had an arrow in his shoulder and two in his chest. Dan dismounted and walked to him. *He put up a hell of a fight,* Dan mumbled noticing all the shell casings lying by him. He picked one up. *Damn Comanche have at least one Henry now,* he mused.

The patrol arrived and the men sat looking at the dead bodies, especially the little girl. As they prepared the bodies for burial, Dan could sense their anger and hatred. He knew when a man hated and got mad enough it could be a good thing-sometimes. Most of the time though, rushing in to a fight all keyed up with hate could get you and your buddies killed because you weren't thinking straight.

It was almost full dark when they finished their dismal work and Dan led them a quarter mile away to make camp. The dead man had a nice place and had been lucky enough to have found water. The patrol replenished their tepid water in their canteens with fresh, cool water from the man's well.

With no fire to give them away the men ate cold biscuits and jerky. The only good thing, they could drink their fill of the fresh water and refill the canteens in the morning before they hit the trail. While eating, the talk among the men was mostly of hate and what they were going to do to those murdering savages; Dan listened till he had enough.

He stood up and walked over to where he stood in front of the three privates that were doing most of the talking. Squatting down he started talking. "Let me try and set your thinking straight," he said trying to smile and not show the disgust he had from listening to the men talk. "These men we are trailing are no different than you and me, they just have different values on things. For the most of us we were raised in a home by parents that taught the good Book and what was right and what was wrong. We were taught certain virtues like respect for other people and that taking a human life was wrong. The Indian, whether

it's Comanche, Apache, or any other tribe has no such
virtues. They were raised with the belief that all strangers
were enemies; all white men want nothing more than to kill
them and take away their homeland which as you know is
basically true. They are fighting men; that is what the
warrior does-they were raised to fight. We look up to our
politicians, presidents, and certain high ranking officers
that were war heroes. The Indian looks up to, gives all his
respect to, the best fighting men in their tribe. They have a
belief in life after death. It's different than ours in certain
ways. They believe they will meet their enemies there and
that when you die you enter this magical place as you leave
the real world. So why leave an enemy with hands that can
shoot an arrow or a gun or eyes that can see you and track
you down. That is the reason for most mutilations of their
enemies. Sometimes however they torture their enemies for
other reasons. The longer it takes for a man to die they
believe that mans strength will go into their bodies. That's
the main reason they will kill a coward quickly because no
strength will be gained from him."

There was a silence among the men for a few
seconds then one, a private named Jackson uttered a remark
that made all of them laugh and even Dan cracked a smile.

"If that's true I will tell you one thing for sure. If the situation arises to where there is no hope of living I'll start screaming like a woman so they will just spit on me and kill me quick."

When things quieted down Dan stood up. "I have lived with the Apache as Tye did. I have had them in my home when I was young. My friends were Apache boys my age. I have been fighting then now for fifteen years. The very Apaches that I use to visit with and who came to my home are the same ones who killed my parents and my sister, and Tye's father, but Tye and me don't hate them; we understand them. You can't hate someone just because their way of thinking is different from yours. Ya'll think about it and you'll see I'm right. Another thing, you men go off half cocked and full of hate, you'll make a mistake that will get you killed and maybe your buddy also." He turned to walk away and then turned back and chuckled. "Don't let them take you prisoner Jackson. If worse comes to worse, just save one shell for yourself." Dan walked away and sat down by a smiling Corporal Absher and Sergeant Carter. "What are you two grinning about?"

Carter spoke up. "Listening to those men awhile ago we wondered how long it would take you to make Tye's virtue speech."

Dan chuckled. "I guess you two have heard it a few times from Tye. I don't recall seeing those three on any patrols before so I thought I would teach them the gospel according to Tye." He laughed again.

"I guessed it worked," Absher said. "They sure have toned down their talk."

Lieutenant Farley stuck the last bit of jerky in his mouth and said. "First time I heard it too Dan. Very impressive speech."

Dan looked over his shoulder at the men and smiled. "We're going to start early. Let's get some sleep."

Chapter Eight

After a hard ride and a short camp the Frazier's were a mile or so from Brackett an hour after the sun broke the eastern horizon. They were surprised no posse or patrol had been seen following them, but Cole figured they were coming and they had better not tarry too long in this miserable excuse for a town. They split up and would come into the town from different directions since if anyone from Uvalde came they would be looking for three men together.

Each would take his horse to the blacksmith shop to get new shoes put on and then mosey casually to the nearest place to eat. They would meet there but sit separately, showing no acknowledgement of each other. Cole stepped down from his horse and walked up to the man holding a large hammer he had been using to flatten out a shoe.

"I've came a good ways and wondered if you might re-shoe my horse?"

The man glanced at Cole then struck the glowing shoe he was working on with a hammer. Cole. "How soon?" he asked spitting a stream of tobacco that barely missed Coles boot.

Cole felt the anger rise as he looked at the tobacco spit near his boot, but let it pass and nodded. "This morning."

The man nodded. "Be ready about half past nine."

"Thanks," Cole said. "Can you give him some water and grain too?"

"Be twenty-five cents extra," The man replied. "

"That's fine," Cole said. "Is there a place open this early a man might find some food?"

The smithy nodded. "Next street over and down a block you'll find the Sargent Hotel. It's a stage stop and the food is usually good."

Cole tipped his hat. "Obliged."

Over the next thirty minutes Ben and Jud left their horses to be shoed. The last horse, Jud's would be ready by noon. Each had gotten direction to the nearest restaurant,

The Sargent Hotel. Arriving separately, they sat at different tables. They saw that Cole was just about through eating. As they got their coffee Cole stood up and paid for his meal and then loud enough for the brothers to hear ask directions to the nearest saloon. The store owner told him that Jim's Place was the cleanest. He thanked the man and without looking at his brothers strode out of the hotel knowing they had heard where he would be.

~~

Many miles northwest of Brackett Quanah sat on his great paint and looked at the Rio Grande River in the dim early morning light. This river separated him from what he was after, the Apache women and Apache horses. Not knowing this country he had sent scouts up and down the river to find a crossing. Where he sat now was only cliffs much to steep for the horses. He and his men were sky lined where they were so they quickly reined their ponies around and went back down the slope to wait on their scouts return.

Across the river, Yahzie, hidden behind some thick junipers, had seen the Comanche and smiled. He knew there was only one crossing for miles in any direction. To get there, the Comanche would have to go through the canyon the Apache had recently named the Canyon of the

Dead. He would have a surprise waiting for them there. He had convinced over a hundred warriors about the coming Comanche. He figured a hundred or so Apaches would be enough to handle a hundred and fifty or even two hundred Comanche; especially with surprise on their side.

He jumped on his pony and rode down river to where he had left his band of warriors. His plan was to wait until the Comanche scouts had rode through the canyon going back to Quanah to tell him of the crossing they had found and then he would set up the ambush. He would have thirty warriors under blankets with dirt over them that would rise up among the Comanche and surprise them. He would have thirty or so in the arroyo that ran fifty yards to the east that would charge as soon as the men came up from the ground. The rest would be on the rocky, west side of the canyon with their Henrys. He figured the Comanche would break for the protection of the rocks. His warriors would wait till they were close before rising from the rocks to fire. He smiled at the thought of the great Quanah Parker's scalp hanging on his lance. This was his one chance to redeem himself to his people for his earlier failure against the bluecoats at the place his people now called the Canyon of the Dead because of the great number of warriors and soldiers killed in the fight there.

The small detachment of soldiers had left their camp well before daylight. Farley had questioned Dan about not being able to see the Comanche tracks in the dark.

"I know about where they are going. We will be close to their trail when it's light enough to see. They rode with no more words spoken. The only sound that broke the morning stillness was the horse's hooves occasional striking rocks, an occasional snort from one of the mounts, along with the squeaking of saddles.

Two hours later as dim light of dawn was approaching and one could actually see the ground, the lieutenant shook his head. Just to his right, not ten yards away was the clear trail of many unshod ponies just as Dan said. He heard a couple of the men behind him make remarks about the tracks also. *Dan's good. Not Tye maybe, but he's a close second,* he mused.

Farley glanced over his shoulder at the men following him. He knew Absher and Carter were experienced Indian fighters, but the others he wasn't sure about. He knew Sims and Dean had been in a few scrapes and Jansen, well he was another story. He had heard about the number of times he had been busted back in rank and the number of times he had been in the guardhouse for various things. Jansen had a hard time getting along with, as he would say, smart-ass young lieutenants that don't know their ass from a hole in the ground. He'd been known to strike a couple with his fist for giving stupid orders that was going to get men killed. It had happened once here at Fort Clark and Major Thurston asked him if he like being a private in this mans army. He told Major Thurston that he did so and politely asked him not to promote him again. All the officers knew about his attitude, but he was a first class fighting man and a soldier through and through. If given a choice, they would all want him as a member of their patrol. Farley smiled when a thought crossed his mind. *I'll just have to be careful about giving stupid orders.*

Dan had reined in and dismounted. He kneeled on the ground and stuck a stick in a pile of horse dung. Pulling it out and looking at it, he realized they had made up a hell of a lot of time. They were no more than a few hours behind the Comanche, probably six to eight at the most.

He stood up and looked west, toward Mexico. He was trying to remember the lay of the land around the Rio Grande here. He knew it ran through deep canyons there for miles with little chance of a safe descent to the river from the canyon rims. He was still turning things over in his mind when the patrol rode up.

Lieutenant Farley walked to Dan and started to sit on a flat rock when a sudden buzzing noise startled everyone followed by a scream of pain. Dan looked away from the horizon where he had been looking when he heard the buzz. He saw the rattler strike the lieutenant just below the knee and above his boots. Farley had his pistol out and was squeezing the trigger when Dan stopped him.

"Don't shoot lieutenant! Don't shoot!" He hollered. He sure didn't want a gunshot alerting any Comanche if they happen to be close by. He grabbed a stick and pulled the rattler out from under the rock it had went back under and pinning the snakes head down with it, cut his head off with a quick flick of his Bowie. Farley had holstered his pistol and was holding his calf with both hands, his face twisted in pain.

"I figure at least one of you men has some rot-gut stashed. I need it now," Dan said. A few seconds later a bottle was handed to him. He had split the lieutenant's pants and took the bottle. He looked up and wasn't surprised to see it was Jansen. '"Thanks, Jansen," he said. He wiped the blade of his Bowie on part of the officer's pants and then poured some of the whiskey on his hands and on the blade. This is gonna hurt some lieutenant."

"Just get it over with, "Farley answered. "Sure as hell can't hurt more than it does now."
Dan cut an X on each fang mark and placing his mouth over the wound sucked, then spit out the blood and hopefully some of the poison. He repeated the scenario two more times and then poured whiskey on it before wrapping it with a piece of a clean shirt the lieutenant had in his saddle bags. He washed his mouth out with some of the whiskey spitting it on the ground. He handed the half empty bottle back to a surprised Jansen.

Dan looked up at Jansen who was a little worried about having the bottle. Dan smiled and said, "It didn't surprise me none that it was you who had the bottle. Every top notch soldier I have ever known took a swig now and then. The lieutenant was hurting so bad he probably didn't notice so put it back in your saddle bags and don't get it out again on this patrol. If the lieutenant remembers the whiskey I will tell him I had it in my saddle bags for emergencies like this."

"Thanks Dan. I won't forget it." He walked over and put the bottle in his saddle bag.

Dan turned to Sergeant Arnold. "I need a couple stout limbs for a travois. We probably need to send a man with the lieutenant back to the fort for medical help."

"Do you know where the Comanche's are crossing for sure.?"

"About ninety percent sure-why?

"I was just thinking. We need to send a man to the Pecos and Rio Grande Junction to meet with the column from the fort. If I know the major like I think I do, he will have a medical officer and ambulance going along with it. We're sorter short on men so I thought maybe we could send the message with the lieutenant and not have to send a man to the fort with him and another to the junction with directions as to where we will be. The lieutenant can get the medical attention there."

Dan thought for a moment. "Good thinking sergeant. Find a man and that's what we will do." He put his hand on Arnold's shoulder and smiled. "I should have thought of that. Tye told me you were a hell of a soldier and was always thinking."

Twenty minutes later the men gathered around the travois Farley lay on. Dan picked up a stick and squatted beside Farley. I need to draw a map so you will understand where we will be and relay it to the column you will meet.

"About ten or so miles there," he said pointing with the stick toward the west, "is the Rio Grande and Mexico." He drew a crooked line on the ground. "This is the river and we are about here." He drew an 'x' on the ground. He waved the stick over the line representing the river. "For miles up and down the river there is no way a man can cross with a horse. The cliffs are high and steep. No way could a horse get down without chancing a broke leg." Right here," he marked an 'x' on the river, "is the only place man and horse can cross safely." He stood up and the men followed suit. Dan looked toward Mexico for a few seconds then turned back to the men.

"I'm betting the Comanche don't know this country and when they come to the river and see there was no way to get down, Quanah will make camp and send scouts up and down the river looking for a place. This is going to take a little time because if you go to the point where I think they are, it's twenty miles down stream to the crossing. That's forty miles round trip for the scout, almost a full day even for an Indian.

, Five minutes later the patrol headed toward the Rio Grande and Farley was lying on the travois headed toward a meeting with the column from Fort Clark.

~~

The whole town of Bracket had turned out to watch the troops leave. They had never seen that many before and every man wondered what the hell was going on. It took ten minutes for all the men to get across the bridge over Los Moras Creek.

Captain McClellan led the troops along with First Lieutenant Bannock, First Sergeant Arnold, and five line sergeants including Zeb Cates. Also there were four corporals, two Farriers (horseshoers and veterinarians), two buglers, an ambulance and medical staff, and about seventy privates. Close to ninety men in all. His orders were to get to the junction of the Pecos and Rio Grande Rivers as quickly as possible.

Among the men watching the troops leave was the Frazier's.

"Pretty impressive," Ben chuckled.

"Makes a man wonder what's going on Cole said. "They're headed out of town the same direction we are heading." He rubbed the back of his neck while watching the parade of soldiers. "We need to see if there's trouble between here and the border before we go. We don't want to run into any damn Apaches."

Chapter Nine

Dan topped a hill and immediately reined his mount around moving quickly back down the slope. He had seen three Indians trotting their ponies in the canyon below him. He hoped they had not seen him. Taking the field glasses from his saddlebag he dismounted and quickly made his way up the slope to the crest. Lying on his belly behind some sage he looked through the glasses at the floor of the canyon where he had saw the Indians. Focusing on them he knew they had not seen him for they were still trotting their ponies. He could tell by their dress they were not Apache. *Comanche. I was right. These are scouts heading back to the main bunch to tell them they found the crossing.* He watched them till they were out of sight to make double sure they had not seen him and were going to circle around and come in on his backside.

Satisfied they had not spotted him he stood up and as he made his way back down toward his horse he saw Carter and the others riding up.

They had dismounted by the time he reached his mount.

"I saw three Comanche riding in the canyon below go back up river. I figure they found the crossing I mentioned and are headed back to tell Quanah and the rest."

"How long do you think it will be before they come back with the others?" Carter asked.

Dan thought for a minute and looked up at the sun to see about what time it was. "It's almost noon and I figure those bucks had about fifteen miles, maybe twenty to go to reach the main bunch. They weren't in a hurry so I figure they will reach Parker about an hour before sundown and they will head this way in the morning and be through this canyon by around noon or one o'clock. Dan turned and loosened the girth on the saddle. Let's take a thirty minute break and rest the horses."

Private Sims took out his pocket watch his father had given him and looked at the time. It was ten minutes till twelve. *How in hell did that man know it was twelve o'clock?* He looked up at the sun and at his watch, then shook his head. *These damn scouts are amazing,* he mused.

With the horses watered and grazing on the short grass the men sat down and chewed some jerky.

Sergeant Carter turned to Sims. "Go up there and sit behind that sage and keep an eye on the canyon below you."

Sims walked up the hill and sat down. *This is a damn waste of time. I could be down there stretched out like Jansen and Dean is.* He parted the sage and looked at the canyon floor. At first he saw nothing and then he saw movement at the far end of the canyon. Riders, a lot of them were coming into the canyon. He picked up a small rock and threw it at the men below him. Dan and Carter looked up at him. He motioned for them to come up to him. Dan grabbed his field glasses and both men went to where Sims sat.

Squatting behind the sage bushes, Dan looked where Sims pointed. He raised his glasses to get a better look. It was Yahzie and close to a hundred warriors.

"Apaches," he said in a low voice. "That's Yahzie leading them."

"What are they going to do? Carter asked.

"Lets wait and see," Dan answered.

As they watched the Apache stopped at the narrowest part of the canyon and begin scratching out shallow holes in the ground. "What the hell are they doing?" Sims asked.

Dan chuckled. "They are going to give the Comanche an Apache surprise party."

"Are they going to do what I think they are?" Carter mumbled.

"Yep." Dan said.

"What in the hell are you two talking about?" Sims questioned.

"They are digging holes for some of the men to lie in." Dan answered. "They will lay in the hole with a blanket over them. The others will cover them with dirt and rocks so the Comanche won't see them till they are right on top of them."

"They just gonna lie there till they come?" Sims wondered out loud.

" No, not yet, but they could. You'll learn Sims, if an Apache don't slit your throat and take your scalp first, that nothing in the world has more patience than an Apache when they are waiting to kill someone." Sims placed his hand on his throat and swallowed thinking about a knife and his throat. Dan smiled at the young private. "I'll watch awhile sergeant. Why don't you and Sims go down to the others."

After studying the terrain by memory he knew that Yahzie knew the Comanche had to come this way to get to the crossing. This way or take another route that would add at least another day. He figured the Comanche's lust for blood and women was pretty high and they probably wanted to get to it as fast as possible. He looked back down at the Apaches working feverishly to prepare the ambush. He thought about the Comanche. "Their mistake," he mumbled. He scooted back down the hill to the others.

Dan walked over to his horse and tightened the saddle girth and stepped into the saddle.

"Be back in a hour or so."

"Where are you going?" Carter asked.

"To talk to Yahzie."

"Tal..Talk to Yahzie-you crazy?" Carter stammered out as the other men stood up looking at the scout like he had a loose screw or something.

"Apaches ain't gonna kill a man that comes into their midst of his own free will and is peaceable." He reined his sorrel around and started up the slope. He looked back and smiled. "At least that's what Tye told me once." He topped the hill and started down the other side.

The Apaches spotted him at once and several mounted their ponies and raced toward him. He held out hands to each side. They were around him in a few seconds. When the dust settled, Dan was looking at Yahzie.

"It is good to see Yahzie made it back to his people in time." Dan was feeling a little nervous and the hairs on the back of his neck were tingling since the Apaches had completely encircled him. He stared at Yahzie, showing no fear, at least on the outside. "We need to make talk."

The Apache nodded and slid off his pony. Dan stepped from the saddle and both men squatted before each other. Yahzie had not spoken to him yet only a few words to his men. *Probably telling them not to kill me-not yet anyway.*

` "I see where the great warrior Yahzie is planning to meet the Comanche. This is good. It is better to carry the fight to your enemy than to wait on them to attack you."

Finally, Yahzie spoke. "It is good to see you my friend. Much brave of you to come in like this. He waved his arms in a circle. There is not a brave here that would not like to have the honor of counting coup on you before killing you."

Dan spoke loudly in his best Apache. "I trust the Apache is an honorable people and would not kill a man who comes in peace among them. A man who wants to help them in their fight against the Comanche."

Yahzie smiled. "Well spoken my friend. Now what is it you want?"

"I see what you are doing and I know that the Comanche have to come through this canyon to reach the crossing. I should have a large troop of men here in the morning sometime. I will close off the canyon after the Comanche pass and if they try to escape your ambush by running back the way they came, we will be there to stop them. If they learn they cannot come down here in Apache land and escape alive, they won't be back and things will be as before between your people and mine."

"It is good," Yahzie said. He stood up and spoke to the braves around him repeating what Dan said. They began yelling and waving their rifles and bows.

Yahzie raised his arms and they quieted down. You have made a few friends here," Yahzie said to Dan. "Not all, but a few. That's a beginning."

The two warriors faced each other and each placed a hand on the others shoulder. "Tomorrow." Yahzie said. Dan nodded and one of the braves handed him the reins to his horse. He mounted and rode away, not looking back. The hairs still stood up on the back of his neck and he half expected a bullet in the back.

"That crazy son-of-a-bitch made it out alive. I'd never believed it if I haven't seen it," Absher said.

Carter was beside Dan before Dan had a chance to rein to a complete stop. "You crazy son-of-a-b…" he stopped talking and laughed. "That had to be the craziest thing I ever saw in my whole miserable life."

Dan dismounted. "To tell you the truth sergeant, that was the craziest thing I ever did."

"What happened."

"Right now, as hard as it is to believe, we sorter have a peace treaty with the Apache-at least those in the canyon there."

"What did you tell them?" Absher asked.

"That we should have more troops tomorrow. If we do, we will block the Comanche's attempt to escape their ambush."

"You did what?" Carter exclaimed loudly not believing what he just heard. "You expect the army to help the Apache!"

"Hear me out sergeant. If the Comanche figure they can come down to this part of Texas any damn time they want, we will be fighting them as well as the Apache. If this excursion by Quanah down here turns into a disaster, they won't be back. Yahzie and the Apache know this is true. Afterwards, things will turn back to normal."

"This is a one day truce then."

"Exactly. I just hope Lieutenant Farley meets a large troop headed this way."

"That's a lot of if's and hope's," Absher said.

"Well if things don't go as planned, the five of us will have close to two hundred Comanche and a hundred Apache warriors running all around us." Dan answered smiling.

"That's a pleasant thought," Absher said.

"I need to relieve myself before I dirty my damn pants," a nervous Private Dean mumbled as he headed for the bushes.

~~

Back in Brackett the Frazier's were in Jim's Place finishing off a round of drinks. They had found that the troops were headed up the Rio Grande so there was no trouble due west toward Mexico. Jud had come back with their newly shod horses. As was their custom, the horses were in back of the saloons they frequented, not in front tied to the hitching rails. This habit was about to save their lives.

Chapter Ten

Cole and his brothers were sitting in Jim's having their last beer before hitting the trail. Each looked up when the bat-winged doors of Jim's opened and four soldiers walked in, one an officer. The officer headed straight to Jim, the owner of the place. Jim, recognizing the lieutenant from previous visits smiled.

"Lieutenant Mason. Good to see you, but what brings you to Brackett from Uvalde?"

Cole and his brothers looked at each other and all three rested their hands on the butts of their Colts.

"Chasing some killers, Jim. They shot up a saloon in Uvalde. Killed the sheriff and a deputy. I think they are the same ones that robbed a bank in San Antonio, ambushed a posse that was chasing them and killed all but two of them."

"Sounds like they are bad news, Lieutenant. Any idea what they look like?"

Mason nodded. Two are stocky with beards and the younger one is slender." Jim's eyes went to the table where the three outlaws sat, but did it quickly and he didn't think the three noticed

They did and all three pulled their guns, knocking over their chairs as they did. Lieutenant Mason and the soldiers turned toward the commotion. The outlaw's gun fired almost as one and then fired again. The noise inside the confined room was deafening and thick smoke lay heavy. As they fired the second shots all three men headed to the back door, slamming it shut just as the shotgun Jim kept under the bar blasted with both barrels blowing the door off its hinges.

Soldiers rushed in from outside, their Springfield's cocked and ready. Jim laid the shotgun on the counter quickly realizing they could shoot him accidently thinking he had shot the Lieutenant and the others. They quickly saw that two of their friends were dead and the Lieutenant had a hole in his shoulder and a nasty burn across the side of his head. The other trooper appeared to have some lead in his shoulder.

"What happened?" a sergeant demanded while holding his gun aimed straight a Jim's chest.

Jim held his hands where the sergeant could see them. "The three men ya'll are after were in here. They shot the soldiers and I fired my shotgun at them as they went out the door."

The sound of running horses could be heard back of the saloon.'

"Someone fetch a damn doctor," the sergeant shouted. "He turned to the remaining five soldiers, "Get to your horses. We're gonna run those bastards down." He checked on the lieutenant; saw he was unconscious, but alive. He looked at Jim. "Take care of him and the wounded trooper." He pointed his Springfield at the unconscious Mason. "Tell the lieutenant where we went."

Jim nodded and then turned to one of his customers. "Bill, get on your horse and ride to the post hospital and fetch a doctor pronto." He looked at some of the other customers that had been too stunned to move. "Larry, George, ya'll get over here and help me get the two wounded on the bar so I can look at them till the doc arrives."

In all the confusion besides being in a hurry to put distance between the town and them, the outlaws headed out of town on the first street they came to. A few minutes later they slowed their mounts to take stock of the situation. They didn't have time because they heard horses, and looking back saw the soldiers coming fast.

Cole knowing his horse was a little winded after the run quickly dismounted and grabbing the reins of his other horse with one hand and the horse's mane with the other, swung up on top bareback. His brothers did the same. Being old southern boys, they had grown up riding this way so it wasn't a problem. They kicked their horses into a gallop and then a hard run. Looking back, Cole saw the soldiers falling back as their mounts were giving out. He smiled and had his horse slow down to an easy lope that the horses could hold for awhile. He still hadn't realized he was going north on the Old Military Road, not west on the Old mail Road that went toward Mexico.

Tye's home on the fort was a good half mile from Jim's place in Brackett. He had not heard the pistol shots from inside the saloon, but did hear the boom of the shotgun. He figured someone was hunting birds and forgot about it. It was thirty minute later when a private sent by

Major Thurston to fetch him when he learned of the shooting.

It took him less than ten minutes to get to Jim's. He saw Major Thurston and the fort's doctor as he walked through the doors. They were at the bar where two soldiers lay with doc working on them. He saw two more lying on the floor obviously dead.

"What happened?' Tye asked walking up beside the major who was standing back from the bar giving doc room to move from one man to the other. He looked at the face of the officer and was shocked. "MASON,' he shouted and rushed to the wounded man's side. He was relieved to find his friend awake. "What the hell, Lieutenant. What's going on?"

Mason forced a smile. "Looks like a damn cowboy almost did what the Apaches been trying to do-get my scalp."

Tye looked at doc and the surgeon nodded that he was going to be okay. He placed his hand on top of Masons. "Doc says it looks like you're gonna live."

Two of my men are dead and the others are chasing those bastards."

"Who are they?"

"Don't know for sure, but the word was they fit the description of the Frazier brothers that robbed some banks in Arkansas a few weeks back killing several people include a little girl. They robbed a bank four days ago in San Antonio and killed a marshal and two deputies as well as a teller in the bank and the banks owner. Another teller was severely beaten."

"Sounds like a bad bunch."

"That's not all Tye. They ambushed the posse chasing them and killed the sheriff and twelve men in the posse."

"Three men did that!"

"The brothers had three other men with them, but they were killed in the ambush. Word was that they might have been killed by the brothers which would up their shares quite a bit." He grimaced as the doc moved his wounded shoulder. "I heard some gossip about you becoming a lawman. Any truth to that rumor?"

Tye smiled. "It's true Lieutenant. I'm a deputy U.S. Marshal."

"Yeah-much to the chagrin of me and a hell of a lot of soldiers," Thurston added.

"Well I be damned."

"As a marshal I'd better get on theirs and your men's trail. I'll see you later Lieutenant." Tyr turned and headed out the door and on to his house. Twenty minutes later he was on Sandy, headed north on the Old Military Road.

~~

The Comanche had not shown themselves as of yet. Dan was glad he had miscalculated their arrival by three hours because the column led by McClellan had not arrived until shortly after one p.m. Dan quickly filled in the captain on what was going on and about his talk with Yahzie.

McClellan chuckled. "That's sounds like something Tye would promise. I guess he's taught you well."

Dan smiled and exhaled a breath of relief. He hadn't been sure how the captain would take to helping the Apaches. "See if you think my plan will work? The canyon where the trap is set is just over that hill," he said nodding toward it. " We will leave maybe fifteen men up there in case the Comanche try and get away by going up the slope instead of back the way they came. At the first sound of the attack by the Apaches, we will ride to the mouth of the canyon with the rest of the men and block their escape that way."

McClellan nodded his head and laughed. "I can't wait to see Thurston's face when he reads my report of how we helped the Apache."

Dan chuckled. "Glad it's you giving the report and not me." Both men sat down to wait until their sentries spotted the Comanche coming.

~~

Damn cavalry is gonna flounder those horses, Tye mused as he trailed the outlaws and the soldiers. *They're running way too hard to hold that pace for very long.* He held Sandy to a canter, staying in the road, but watching both sides for any tracks leaving it. He wasn't gaining ground yet, but he would when both the soldiers and outlaw horses were tiring. He knew the soldiers mounts would first because they were running harder than the outlaws.

Twenty minutes later he saw the soldiers standing beside the road. Their horses stood with heads down, completely spent. Reining Sandy in he placed his hands on the pommel of his saddle. "You men should have known better than to run those horses that way, especially in this heat." He looked at the horse's sides, heaving and looking like they had been given soap baths with all the lather on them.

"Who the hell are you?" The sergeant asked.

Before Tye could tell him, a private spoke up. "That's Tye Watkins from Clark, Sergeant."

"That true?" The sergeant asked.

Tye nodded. "I'm Tye, and like I said sergeant, you shouldn't have run those horses into the ground."

The sergeant hung his head and then looked up at Tye. "I kno'd that. But that Lieutenant Mason was a good officer and I just sorter lost it when I seen what those son-of-bitches did, him lying there all shot up like that. Is he...?"

"He's not dead sergeant. He was talking to me before I left." The other men perked up at that news as well as the sergeant. "The doc said he was gonna live." Tye was glad his friend was well thought of by the men he led. "You men just lead your horses on foot for awhile back toward Brackett. They should be okay after while-at least good enough to carry you into town if you take it easy."

"You staying after them?" the sergeant asked.

"I'll bring them back-dead or alive, but I will get them." He nudged Sandy into a lope again heading north while the soldiers turned into infantry and headed south.

~~

"Sir," Carter said to McClellan and then nodded toward the crest of the hill where the sentry was. The sentry was motioning for the captain to come up and take a look. Dan and McClellan eased up the slope to the crest, took off their hats and knelt down behind s thick sage beside the private.

Below them and to their left was the largest gathering of warriors McClellan had ever seen. " God Almighty!" he whispered. "There must be close to two hundred."

"Yahzie and his warriors are outnumbered about two to one," Dan whispered back.

"They don't stand a chance in hell," the young private said.

Dan looked at him and smiled. "You fought the Apache before?'

"No sir. I just got here a month ago."

"Well, get ready for your first lesson in Apache warfare." He looked back at the Comanche hoard. "That has to be Quanah on that big paint."

McClellan swung his field glasses to the front of the mass of warriors centering in on the warrior on the paint. Noticing the fancy head dress of eagle feathers he mumbled. "Most likely."

"They will be in the trap in five or so minutes, Captain. We'd better get in position."

McClellan nodded and the three of them backed down the slope a few feet before standing up and hurrying down to the men.

"Corporal Absher."

"Yes sir."

"You take A and C patrol and spread out along that ridge up there where we just were. If the Comanche make a break up that slope toward you-stop them."

"Yes sir," Absher said giving a quick salute and then turning around, barked, "A and C patrols on that ridge up there with me and stay out of sight. Don't get yourself sky lined." Men were quickly picketing their mounts and heading up the slope following Absher.

"Get the rest of the men mounted, Lieutenant," he said turning to Lieutenant Bannock.

"Yes sir," the young lieutenant answered and giving a quick salute, turned to the men. "Mount up." Mounted, they followed McClellan around the hill to the mouth of Dead Man's Canyon to wait for the Apache ambush.

Chapter Eleven

Tye rode in the middle of the Old Military road so he could see both sides of the road looking for any tracks leaving it. He was paying particular attention to the left side because he figured sooner or later the men would head toward Mexico. It was up-hill for now as the road was heading into the mountains. Tye smiled as a thought crossed his mind. *Old Buff always laughs when we Texans talk about the mountains in Texas. He says the biggest he has seen here wouldn't even be a foothill in the Rockies.*

After an hour of steady climbing Tye was about to halt to give Sandy a breather when he saw the tracks. Three set of tracks led away from the road to the west-toward Mexico. Dismounting, he knelt to study the tracks closer so he would be able to recognize them later. A horse's tracks are like a man's footprint-each is individual and different. If a man know what to look for he can pick out a certain horse's tracks from several other horses tracks. One horse had a front hoof that turned slightly out and he noticed all of them appeared to be freshly shod.

He followed the tracks until the sun began its decent behind the hills. He knew there would be a full moon tonight so he stopped to give Sandy some water and let him rest till the moon came up. He would be on the trail again then. *They won't expect a visitor tonight,* he mused. *I'm positive they knew what happened to the soldiers that were chasing them. That's why they appear to be in no hurry.* He smiled- *their mistake.*

Sitting on a rock chewing jerky he thought about the lay of the land up here. The last time he was in this area was when he was chasing Yancey Cates. Thinking about it he knew he needed to end it tonight because once the outlaws hit the flat country west of here they'll light a shuck fast for Mexico and will be hard to catch up with.

It was full dark and the moon had started its trek across the night sky when he walked over to Sandy and cinched up the girth on his saddle. "I know you were expecting a night of rest ole boy, but we need to catch us some bad men." He mounted up and headed west following the tracks by the light of the full moon.

Two miles ahead the three outlaws had finished eating a hot meal of beans and potatoes and were relaxing, drinking coffee.

"Sure looking forward to having a poke with some of those senoritas in Mexico and getting drunk on tequila," Jud said, a broad smile on his face.

"I think we ought to just take the money, buy some land and run some cows and horses," Ben said.

Cole said. "We will have some fun with the girls and probably get drunk, but you're right Ben-we need to be smart with the money. We can get set up pretty good with what we have in them bags."

"Sounds like work to me," Jud said. "Ranching ain't easy you know."

"Nothing worthwhile is Jud," Cole remarked. "Do you think living like we have the last two months is fun; sleeping on the ground, always watching our back trail and can't even go into a town that has a sheriff without chancing what happened in Uvalde and Brackett. Do you call that living?" Neither brother said anything because they knew Cole was right.

"Jud," Cole said. "You go back about a quarter of a mile and make sure no one is on our tail. I'll relive you in a couple hours so don't get trigger happy."

Jud cursed and asked. "Do you really think someone is on our trail? You saw those stupid soldiers' flounder their horses and no one was behind them."

"I did, Jud."Cole answered sharply. "And we are still above ground because we're not dumb or careless. Now do as I say or do I need to just whip your butt," he said standing up and moving toward his little brother.

"Aw hell Cole," Jud said standing up also, "Don't get your bowels in an uproar. I'm going."

"I'll see you in a couple hours," Cole said. "If you see anything just come on back here quick-like. Don't try anything and don't be stupid." Jud didn't answer, just turned his back and walked to his horse.

Cole sat back down and poured him another cup of coffee. "Damn kid is gonna be the death of us Ben."

"He's okay Cole," Ben said. "He's just a kid and will grow up someday."

"If he lives long enough," Cole answered sitting his cup down and stretching. "Let's get a little shuteye. Remember, you need to relieve me about two a.m. or so." Ben nodded and lay down.

Jud had found a good spot to sit and wait on Cole. He remembered this place from when they passed through earlier. A fire long ago had burned all the cedar from the area and now only had sage, patches of grass, and cactus growing. He could look back over his shoulder and see the small fire of their camp about a quarter mile back. He removed some small rocks, smoothed out a place with his hand for his butt, sat down and leaned back against one of the blackened trunks of a maple. He didn't figure anyone would be along their back trail so he figured to get a little shut eye. *Cant' no one follow tracks in the dark no how,* he mused as he closed his eyes. He had picketed his horse behind him where there was a patch of grass.

Tye had dismounted and was holding Sandy reins in his left hand, his Colt in his right. He knew he was no more than a couple hours or so behind the men and leading Sandy, was moving as quiet as possible when he saw the horse on top of the small knoll in front of him. He put his hand on Sandy's nostrils to prevent him from nickering if he caught wind of the horse. Tye turned and back-tracked leading Sandy away from the area to an arroyo he had just passed. As was his habit, he tied Sandy to a bush that if he needed to, could break free. If something happened to him he didn't want Sandy to suffer of thirst because he could not get loose.

He now sat about fifty yards from the horse on the knoll. *That has to be the stupidest thing I have ever saw in my life, tying a horse on top of a hill with a full moon out for all to see.* He chuckled, and moved to his left to skirt the hill and come up from behind the man- or men. He really figured he would find only one man who would be watching their back trail while the others were camped a short distance away.

Stepping lightly he was quickly around the hill and moving up the slope toward the horse. He had put on his Apache moccasin boots and the soft leather soles allowed him to feel any twigs that might snap if he put his weight down on them. He made not a sound as he moved up the hill toward the horse. When he was a few feet away, he comes up from his crouch he had been in and searched the area in front of the horse that had turned his head and looked at the stranger. The horse looked at Tye then dropped his head and went back to nibbling the short grass. Tye could see the shoulders of a man sticking out from behind a burned cedar trunk.

When he was beside the horse he patted him on the neck for few seconds making friends. He didn't want a nicker or snort to alarm the man who sat about ten feet away. Tye didn't want to have to kill him if it wasn't necessary. Moving silently as only a man raised around Apaches could, he reached the spot where the man sat and smiled- the stupid man was breathing heavily, sound asleep.

Tye knelt in front of the sleeping man, holstered his Colt and pulled the Bowie from the sheath in the top of his right moccasin boot. He placed the razor sharp point about six inches from the man's face and cleared his throat. The man's eyes opened and seeing Tye, reached for his pistol. Tye's left hand shot forward and grasped the man's hand in a vice-like grip preventing him from pulling it from the leather.

"Unless you want to try swallowing this Bowie," Tye said, If'n I was you, I wouldn't make a sound or even blink an eye." The man, who Tye had noted couldn't be over twenty years old, nodded. Tye released his hand and lifted the gun from its leather. "Stand up real slow and easy like," he said quietly. He had seen the flickering flames of the small camp fire when he squatted in front of the man a moment ago. He didn't want any noise to alert them.

"What's your name cowboy," Tye asked quietly, and then added. "Speak very quietly." The man didn't say anything. "Your name," Tye repeated but more sternly this time and touched the man's cheek with the point of the Bowie.

"Jud...Jud Frazier," the youngster whispered. Tye nodded and stepped back and smashed a left fist hard into the man's gut and then reversed the Bowie as the man doubled over and brought the butt of the heavy handle down hard on the man's skull. The man collapsed without a sound. Tye walked over to the horse and took a coil of rope off the saddle and cut two short lengths which he used to tie the unconscious man's hands and feet with. He figured the man would be out long enough for him to make the camp and arrest the others.

~~

It had been something none of the soldiers would ever forget seeing, including the scout, Dan August. Dan had been raised along the border and like Tye, had been fighting Apaches most of his life and figured he had seen everything at least once, but today he had witnessed something few white men ever saw; a battle between two warring Indian tribes.

The soldiers, led by Dan and Captain McClellan had spread themselves out along the entrance to the canyon to prevent the invading Comanche escaping the Apache ambush as soon as the first shot was heard. Absher along with A and C troops were spread along the rim to their left. The men on the rim saw the Apaches rise from the earth among the Comanche's firing their rifles and them pistols at point blank range.

The initial barrage was devastating to the Comanche, but the invaders quickly retaliated. Comanche warriors threw themselves off the war ponies onto the Apaches on the ground. War cries from both the Comanche and the Apache filled the air mingling with the screams of the wounded warriors and horses along with the continuous sound of guns blasting away.

As the troopers watched, the savagery of the battle increased as the warriors now fought hand to hand with knives, tomahawks and the ten foot long spears the Comanche carried. In less than a minute all the fifteen or so Apaches were dead, but they had killed a like number of Comanche and wounded several more.

The troopers heard before they saw a large band of Apaches attacking the Comanche from the other end of the canyon. The Comanche warrior on the great paint led his men toward the rocks on the opposite side of the canyon. Many fell from their racing ponies as Apaches fired into them from where they had been hidden among the boulder strewn canyon wall.

The Comanche veered to the right back to the entrance of the canyon where they had come from only to see many soldiers spread along the opening. The war chief led his warriors toward the gently sloping canyon wall that Absher and his men were on. Almost a hundred warriors raced up the slope toward to two troops of blue coats.

"FIRE!" Absher screamed as the first wave of Comanche were no more than fifty yards away. Several were knocked from the ponies as the distance closed between the two groups. The soldiers, knowing they could not reload their Sharps in time, pulled their pistols and another volley at almost point blank range accounted for a few more warriors hitting the rocky slope. The Comanche over run the badly outnumbered troopers firing into the blue clad white eyes as their war ponies rushed past and in some cases leaping over them in their haste to escape the trap. They never slowed their ponies because the Apache, led by Yahzie were right behind them paying no mind to the soldiers as they ran past them.

The trap set by Yahzie and Dan had worked perfectly. The Comanche left thirty nine dead warriors strewn about the canyon floor and on the slope where the soldiers were. No one knew how many were wounded, but the estimates were that many were. The only casualties among the Apache were the fifteen that had been on the ground. Four troopers on the hill were dead and six wounded, all of which would live to fight and possibly die another day which is the plight of all soldiers out here.

Yahzie returned from the chase with the Comanche and dismounting, walked to Dan and Captain McClellan, a huge grin spread across his face. He placed a hand on each of the two men's shoulder and in broken English mixed with Spanish expressed his and the Apache gratitude to the soldiers. He looked at the dead bodies of the soldiers.

"I would like to know their names so they can be remembered by my people of their sacrifice." Both McClellan and Dan were deeply moved by this request and the names were given to the Apache leader.

"My people will not forget your help this day. The Comanche will not come back and for this my people are grateful. However, as we discussed yesterday," the warrior said looking at Dan, "Things between my people and yours will return as before."

Dan nodded his understanding and in Spanish said. "It is so, but your people and my people will have only one enemy to face, not two like we would if the Comanche raid had been successful because they would have been back time and time again."

The Apache warrior leaped onto the back of his pony and nodded his understanding and without another word rode down the slope toward the canyon floor where the butchery of the fallen Comanche dead was taking place. This sight, the sight of heads being hacked off, hands cut off and bodies being disemboweled was something the soldiers would never forget as long as they lived.

Chapter Twelve

Tye was on the edge of the outlaw's camp kneeling behind a thick sage just outside the glow from the small fire. The two men appeared to be asleep, but he decided to wait for a moment to make sure. All was quiet and he damned near jumped out of his skin when a coyote howled that could not be more the a hundred yards away. He chuckled to himself. *These boys here sure ain't Apaches son, so relax and let things come your way and quit being so damned jumpy*

Two minutes later, satisfied both men were asleep; he stood up and drawing his Colt from its leather, walked into camp. Neither man stirred. He positioned himself to where both men were in front of him and said in a cheerful voice, "Time to wake up sleepy-heads." He would instantly learn a lesson that almost cost him his life.

Ben stood up as did Cole, facing Tye. "Who the hell are you?" Cole demanded loudly.

"The U.S. Marshall that's taking you in to be hung." The last word had not come out of his mouth when Ben's gun suddenly appeared in his hand and flame flashed from its barrel. The bullet buzzed past Tye's left ear as his own pistol roared. Ben grunted and dropping his gun, grabbed his right shoulder with his left hand. Tye swung his Colt toward Cole just as the outlaws hand gripped the butt of his pistol.

Cole, looking down at the business end of a cocked forty-five, froze. His eyes went from Tye to his brother and then back to Tye.

"Either fill your hand or unbuckle and let it drop," Tye said, his tone making Cole know it didn't make the marshal any difference which he did. He moved his hand very slowly away from the butt of the Colt and unbuckled his gun belt, letting it fall to the ground.

"Kick it toward me and then sit your butt on the ground with your legs crossed Injun fashion. Cole did as he was told.

"You gonna look at my brother lawman." Tye looked at the man who was in such pain he didn't know-or care what was going on around him.

"I only winged him. Didn't intend to kill him though it would probably have saved the state and me a lot of trouble if I had." He walked over to the wounded outlaw. "Bullet went clean thru," Tye said noticing the exit hole in the back of the man's shoulder. "He's gonna be hurting some, but he'll live to face the hangman."

"You ain't got us back yet. A lot can happen before we get back to that hell hole town of Brackett."

Tye took two quick steps to the man and uncorked a left fist that had all his weight behind it that caught Cole flush on the chin. The blow rocked his head back and he staggered back two or three steps before collapsing to the ground. He wasn't completely unconscious, but his arms and legs didn't seem to respond to what he wanted them to do and his head was spinning like he had been on a three day drunk. Tye quickly strode over to one of the horses and cut two short lengths of rope from the rope on the saddle. When he returned the outlaw had managed to get to his hands and knees.

"On your stomach," Tye said as he pushed the man back to the ground with his boot. He pulled Cole's hands

134

behind his back and tied them securely with one piece of
the rope. He grabbed the man's shirt collar and jerked him
to a sitting position. After tying the still groggy mans feet
together with the second piece of rope he walked over to
the wounded outlaw who was moaning and groaning like a
baby. After making sure he had no other weapons and
picking up the pistol the man had dropped he walked to the
horses and opened one of the saddle bags. In it was more
money than he had ever saw before. He closed that bag and
opened the other and found what he was looking for-a clean
shirt. He walked back to where Ben sat moaning and
rocking back and forth holding his shoulder.

He picked up a bottle of whiskey the men had been
drinking earlier. He squatted in front of the outlaw. "Move
your hand and let me look at the wound. He saw the small
hole that was low on the shoulder well below the shoulder
bone. The hole on the back was larger and nastier looking.

"You done kilt me you sonofabitch," he said
looking at Tye for the first time since the shooting.

"You ain't gonna die," Tye said then added, "At
least not from this wound so quit whimpering like a damn
baby. He pulled the cork from the bottle. "This is gonna
burn some," he said as he poured some whiskey on the hole
in front and then on the one on the man's back. He walked

back to the man's saddle and cut another length of rope, this one about five feet long. He knew it would be damn uncomfortable for the outlaw if he tied his hands behind his back so he tied them in front and then ran the rope to the man's boots and tied his feet together. After checking his knots on both men's ropes he went to get Sandy, the other outlaw and his horse.

Returning with the younger brother he tied Jud securely and placed him between the other two so he could easily see all three at the same time.

Jud looked at Ben and then Tye. "He hurt bad?"

"Nope," Tye answered, "Just a mite painful is all."

"Who are you?"

"Tye Watkins. I'm a U.S. Marshall."

"Never heard of you."

Tye smiled. "Don't reckon there's no reason you should have. Now shut your mouth and get some shuteye." Tye spread his blanket on the ground and lay down. Lying there he reflected on what had happened when he confronted the two men. All he could see was a blur as the outlaws hand drew his gun and fired before Tye could react. *I've never saw a man draw and shoot that quick* he mused. *That's something to remember the next time I pull down on an outlaw. Maybe I had better see about working on my own draw too.* With that thought he drifted off to sleep.

By the time the sun topped the low hills the four men had made their way back to the Old Military Road and were headed south toward Bracket and Fort Clark. The only talking from the three outlaws had been Cole's cursing the youngest for falling asleep and allowing the lawman to capture them. Ben said nothing, just groaned with just about every step his horse took. Tye could appreciate what the man felt like because he had been shot in the shoulder once and had to ride two days before he could get it doctored properly.

He reflected back to the night before when he stripped the gun belt from Ben. He remembered how low the outlaw had wore his gun and the holster was tied down. *Makes sense,* he thought. *If you want to get your gun out quick, the butt is close to your hand and would be easier to draw than it would be high on your hip like me and the soldiers wear ours. You hardly would have to bend your arm to draw and fire. I'm gonna work on that first chance I get.*

His thoughts were interrupted when he saw several men riding toward him on the road-blue clad men. He reined in and waited. There was something familiar about the man in front that had civilian clothes on. The way he sat the saddle and rode was familiar. Suddenly it dawned on him who it was.

"What the hell!" he exclaimed out loud. That's ole Buff leading them soldiers." He kneed Sandy and he and his little troop of outlaws rode forward at a trot much to the chagrin of Ben who was cussing and calling Tye every foul word he could think of. When the two parties met, Tye rode up to Buff and the two shook hands.

What in the world are you doing out here?

Buff sat in the saddle with his hands crossed on the pommel. "Dan hasn't gotten back from patrol and Robert was scouting for a patrol down south. Thurston asked if I would lead these here soldiers and find you. So here I am, back in the saddle again," he added with a huge grin on his face. He looked past Tye to the men. "Looks like you didn't need any help."

Tye grinned. "I would hope all the men I chase down would be this easy." He looked at the soldiers behind Buff and recognized the men from Fort Inge he had seen on the road chasing the Fraziers. He nodded to the sergeant. "Would you mind escorting these three back to the fort?"

"Be more than happy to Tye."

"One's shot up pretty bad and won't be a problem, but watch the other two especially the big man there. That's Cole Frazier. He's the leader of this wolf pack and I've got a feeling would kill you as soon as look at you." He spoke loud enough for the outlaws to hear him.

"Don't you fret over him getting away? If he even looks at me wrong, I'll plug him deader than an old piece of wood. We ain't forgot who he is and what he did to our Lieutenant and friends back in Bracket. We'll make damn sure they get back and hang."

Tye nodded and turned back to Buff. "How's Rebecca and the babies?"

"They're great. Missing you of course." He laughed and added. "You keep gone and them two kiddos just might think old Buff here is their pa."

Tye reached across and placed his hand on Buff's shoulder and smiled. "You just take care of them Buff. Tell Rebecca I miss her and I'll be back soon." He handed the rope to the sergeant that had all three horses tied to it. "They are all yours sergeant." He reined Sandy around and galloped north to find Bloody Jack Gillespie.

Chapter Thirteen

Tye, sitting easy in the saddle on top of a knoll, was looking at something he had only seen two or three times in his life-a herd of buffalo that numbered maybe a hundred counting the calves. It was a beautiful sight. *I can't imagine what a herd of a thousand or ten thousand that use to roam the land would look like,* he mused as he watched the magnificent beasts as they lolled around a water hole, some drinking, some munching on the grass, and others rolling on the ground each raising a dust cloud. A great number of birds were on the ground and on the backs of the animals getting their meal of ticks and other bugs that had found a home in the thick fur of the buffs.

He thought of the stories that Buff had told him of westerners like Kit Carson who had hunted the beast for food for the men building the railroads. When the demand back east for buffalo hides increased it was a profitable business hunting them and sending the hides back east. It was profitable if one could stay alive. The Indian had a special dislike for these hunters. Kit, Billy Dixon and others would make a stand and kill maybe fifty or a hundred or more before having to move. They could kill hundreds in just a few days. The skinners would move in and take the hides and the tongues, leaving the rest for the scavengers. A feeling of remorse overcomes Tye as he reflected on the millions of Buffalo killed by these hunters. Killing these great beasts more than any other single thing, led to the downfall of the Redman. The Indian, especially the western and plains tribes, depended on the Buffalo for food, shelter, clothing, and tools.

He stepped down from the saddle and stood beside Sandy, his right hand scratching the horse under the chin. He wasn't going to scare the animals from where he was by getting down and moving around. He was almost a quarter mile away and what little breeze there was, was in his face. Buffalo had poor eyesight, but they had a great sense of smell.

He watched the magnificent beasts for ten more minutes before he decided he had better get back to the task at hand. Mounting Sandy he gently nudged him in the flanks with the heel of his boot and they were moving north again.

~~

Jack Gillespie sat on his bed in the bunk house of his brother's ranch. It was a small ranch, but it had lots of promise to be something special with a few years of hard work. Jacks older brother, Jarrod, had started the ranch shortly after the big war. Neither brother knew if the other survived or not since Jarrod fought for the Union and Jack for the Confederacy. Jack had accidently overheard some cowboys talking about different ranches they had worked while he was in a saloon in Brackett a few days ago. One of the ranches mentioned was owned by a man named Jarrod Gillespie. Jack knew the odds of the man being his brother were slim and none but he had nothing to lose by checking it out. His venture into Mexico could wait a few days. When he found the ranch he was as surprised as his brother when he rode into the yard in front of the house

The two spent hours talking about the war and what had transpired since. Before turning in for the night Jarrod startled Jack by asking if he was the Jack Gillespie known as Bloody Jack. He had heard some stories from one of the hands that worked for him who had recently came from San

Antonio and brought a couple newspapers with him. The description in the paper fit his brother perfectly.

Jack admitted being the same and went on to explain that bad luck just seemed to follow him. Everywhere he went it seemed somebody died. He lied and said none of the events was his fault that it was just matter of him being in the wrong place at the wrong time. He told the truth about the rancher and bank teller in San Antonio, but explained that it was a spur of the moment thing and he intended to hurt no one. Jack had become a good actor and liar lately and actually convinced Jarrod he was truly sorry for what had happened. He didn't bring up the whore and men in Fort Worth he killed or the killings in Houston or the more recent in Uvalde and Brackett.

He sat on the bed pondering his past and wondering about his future. He was a young seventeen year old teenager when he joined the Confederacy a year and a half after the war began. He came out of the war without receiving a single wound-at least not a physical wound. He saw so much misery and death while fighting for the South that he was calloused as far as watching people die-or killing them for that matter.

He had ridden with Quantrill for a short period and witnessed and participated in things that would shape his mental outlook on what was right and what was wrong. What he wanted was right and if anyone got in his way he would kill them. He had practiced long hours on his draw and though he was probably not the fastest around, he was a close second and his steel nerves and his ability to hit what he aimed at made up for any short comings he had with his draw.

He had built a reputation in the Fort Worth, Texas area of being just that, quick with a gun and not one to mess with. Since the war he had killed six men in fair fights in the streets of that city. He was likable, but quick tempered, especially if he had been drinking.

He was popular with the ladies what with him being six foot tall, well built, striking blue eyes and long, straw colored hair that reached his shoulders. Being a ladies' man had gotten him into some tight spots before and two of the men he had killed were over the attention of one of the ladies in Sadie's Place. He was sweet on Josie, one of the working girls there and if he was drinking, which was most of the time, it was best for
one to leave her alone. Of course she wasn't too happy about it as his attention was cutting into her income. She quit mentioning it to him after the second d time he damn near beat her to death for saying anything about it. His

jealousy led to his fleeing Fort Worth for doing just that, beating her to death. The killing of a woman, even if she was a working lady in a saloon, was not tolerated in Texas and he barely escaped the town with his life.

He traveled to Houston where he promptly killed a local patron of a saloon in an argument over a 'lady' that worked there. He was temporarily jailed by Sheriff Madison, but was released a couple hours later when once again, his shooting of the man was considered a fair fight.

A few days later in San Antonio, Jack found himself completely broke, asked to leave the hotel room he had been staying in and did not have enough cash for even one drink. He had sold his horse, saddle, and everything else except the clothes he wore and his Colt and gun belt. He had even sold his Henry repeater. Miserable and irritable, he ambled aimlessly down the street. He found a chair in front of a hardware store and sat down. Looking across the street he watched people going in and out of the First National Bank of San Antonio. The longer he watched people taking money in and some counting their money coming out of the bank, the more irritable he become.

Finally, after watching a man dismount from a fine looking horse and go into the bank he had had enough. He checked his Colt and slid it back into its leather and walked across the street. He entered the bank and after looking around got into the short line of people behind the man he had seen that just walk into the bank.

When the man was at the teller window, the young man behind the counter spoke to the man.

"Good morning Mr. Anderson. What can I do for you?"

"Need to draw some money out for payroll Jimmy, and for some cattle I'm buying," the rancher said.

"How much do you need?"

"Three fifty for the payroll and two thousand for the cattle."

Yes sir Mr. Anderson," the clerk replied. "He counted out the money and handed it to Anderson. "Tell the missus I said hello."

"I'll do just that Jimmy. Thanks."

He turned to leave and found himself looking at the wrong end of a forty-five caliber Colt. "Give me that damn money," Jack demanded.

"Like hell I will you son-of-a-b..." He never finished as Jack shot him right between the eyes and grabbed the wad of cash before the rancher toppled to the floor. He shot Jimmy in the throat when the clerk came up from behind the counter with a pistol. He ran outside and jerking the reins of the rancher's horse loose from the railing, jumped in the saddle and headed out of town. A bullet whizzed by his ear and looking to his right saw the sheriff taking aim again. Jack fired quickly and saw the sheriff spin around and fall to the ground. A few seconds later he had the horse in a full run and the last building of the city was falling behind him.

Townspeople were gathering at the scene to see what had happened. Several were around the fallen officer.

"What happened Sheriff?" Doc Jones asked sitting on the ground holding his friends head in his lap. A quick look at the wound told him that his friend wasn't going to make it. He had seen too many of this kind to think any different.

"D..don't know for sure Doc. Heard shots in the bank, a man came out holding a gun and jumped into the saddle on Dave Anderson's horse." The sheriff's voice was barley a whisper as he struggled for words. Man I arrested yesterday, Jack Gillespie done kilt me. Don't know who else he...". His lips quivered and his eyes set on his friend of ten years, Doc Jones. "Doc...tell my wife I...Doc watched the light in his friends eyes dim and then fade away as Madison's life ended on the street of the town he had protected for ten years. A tear rolled down the doc's cheek as he looked at the crowd around him. He choked out. "You heard the sheriff. It was Jack Gillespie that shot him. Get a damn posse together Tom," he said looking at Tom Blanchard, one of Madison's deputies.

"Doc…Doc," a man hollered from across the street at the bank. Everyone turned their heads. "Doc. There's two more men shot in the bank."

Jack rode the horse as fast and long as he dared without floundering him. He slowed him to a trot and then a walk. He was watching his back trail expecting the posse to be there at any moment. He patted the wad of money he had stuffed in his shirt pocket and chuckled. "Easiest damn money I ever earned," he said out loud and patted the sweaty horse's neck. "Let's see. At cowboy wages of thirty a month I figure I made more in two minutes than I could make in…" he paused while he did some calculating. "Damn, four or five years busting my ass chasing them damn smelly longhorns."

He continued on west on the Old mail Road toward Uvalde, then figured he would go onto Brackett and then Mexico. *From what I have heard from men that's been there two thousand dollars will last a long time there if one doesn't get crazy with the senoritas or get drunk and lose it. Maybe another opportunity for some more easy money will pop up between here and the border.* That thought brought a smile to his face. He gave no more thought to the men he had just killed and families he had destroyed than one would smashing a pesky fly.

Just before dark he reined his horse off the road toward some oak trees a half mile off the road. He figured there was water there and he sure needed some since all he had was what was in the canteen on the horses saddle he had borrowed and it was just about gone. He decided to go ahead and make a cold camp after finding a nice spring there. He rode back to where he left the road and dismounted. He cut a mesquite limb and brushed out his tracks for several yards from the road. He remounted his horse and rode to the spring. He was no pilgrim so he let his horse drink his fill and then moved a hundred yards farther back into the brush. *A man can't be to careful,* he mused. *There' all kinds of bad men out here that would kill and rob you for five dollars.* He chuckled at that thought and lay down for the night.

Jack rode into Uvalde shortly after noon the following day. Hungrier than a she- wolf with pups he inquired where a man might find something to eat. Like most folks he was directed to the local restaurant and found the food good. With a full belly of steak, potatoes, beans, and fresh baked bread he left the hotel to find a saloon and maybe a card game. It was early, but knowing cowboys and their love of poker he figured he could find one.

He was surprised to find three games going on in the first saloon he walked into. He bought a bottle and sat down at a table close to two of the games so he could watch and see who had the 'hot' hand. At the nearest table he watched a man dressed in black pants and coat, white shirt, string bow tie, and a flat crowned black hat. He watched him deal with great skill with hands that had not seen manual labor for a long time. A long, thin black cigar protruded from the man's thin lips.. He had a neatly trimmed goatee, a straight nose and dark eyes under heavy eyebrows. Jack sized him up as a professional gambler. The three gents playing with him were obviously hard working cowboys enjoying some time off from pushing cattle and building fences.

Now Jack was about as far from being an angel as one could get; he would rob you and maybe kill you, but he simply could not stand a man who would cheat at cards, especially a man who played poker for a living like this man he was watching probably did. It galled him to watch a professional take the hard earned money of cowboys. As he watched he saw the man deal a card to himself from the bottom of the deck. The man was good and if Jack hadn't been watching him closely, he would have never seen it. He beat one of the cowboys who had bet all he had on three ladies with a full house. The cowboy stood up quickly knocking over his chair in the process and shouted "no one can be that damn lucky all the time."

Jack, from that statement, figured the man had been winning pretty consistently from the cowboys. The gambler asked what the man was implying and the cowboy, pointing a finger at the man said he was a damn worthless card cheat. Now, men in this era might put up with a man who picks up a stray cow that didn't have his brand on it for food and might tolerate a thief, but these men as a whole downright hated a man who cheated at cards. The cowboy standing and pointing his finger at the man in black had everyone in the saloon attention. The other two sitting at the table had scooted their chairs back out of the line of fire which they figured was coming.

The man in black stood up and when he did Jack saw a derringer suddenly appear in his hand. The honest cowboy was going to die if he made a play for his Colt. Jack's Colt was quickly in his hand and when the cowboy's hand dropped toward his Colt, he feathered the trigger of his gun and the noise of the Colt's blast in the room was deafening. The gamblers hand was almost level and pointing at the startled cowboy who was suddenly looking at the twin barrels of the derringer when the heavy slug from Jack's gun struck him in the left ear and blew half of his skull apart on the right side where it exited. After the explosion of Jacks Colt, it was eerily quiet in the saloon as the patrons simply sat or stood where they were and stared at the dead man and at Jack. All of them had seen men killed before in gun or knife fights, but never this quickly, this unexpectedly.

The first man to move was the cowboy who was standing in front of the twin barrels of the gambler's derringer. Walking over to Jack, who still held the smoking Colt in his hand, he offered his hand.

"Want to thank you mister for saving my miserable life."

Jack holstered his gun and shook the man's hand. "You're welcome."

"How…How did you know about the hide-out gun?"

"Been watching him since I sat down. I saw him deal off the bottom to beat your three ladies. I've been around enough of these card sharks to know most of them

have the derringers hid away. They always want the edge
whether its cards or any other thing they do. When I saw
you stand up I slipped my Colt out and watched his hand.
When I saw the gun I fired."

"Well, you sure as hell kilt him deader than an old
door knob. Let me buy you a drink." Just as the two headed
to the bar the bat-winged door opened and the Sherriff and
one of his deputies came in, guns drawn.

Looking around and then at the dead gambler lying
on the floor the sheriff asked what happened. Two or three
men started talking at the same time.

"Ben, you and Jesse shut up. I can only listen to one
of you at a time. He looked at the young cowboy whose life
Jack's quick action had just saved. "Leslie, what
happened?"

Leslie quickly filled the sheriff in on the details.
"The rest of you see it that way too?" He asked. The men
either nodded their heads in agreement or answered yes.
The sheriff holstered his gun and then the deputy. He
looked at the young man who had done the shooting.
"What's your name, son?

"Ben...Ben Wilkinson," Jack said, not wanting to
give the lawman his real name figuring his name had
probably already been sent out on the telegraph.

The old sheriff looked him over and the man fit the description of a thief and killer he had received over the wire yesterday. "Passing through?"

Jack nodded. "Looking for work if any of you know of anyone needing a pretty good hand," speaking loud enough for everyone to hear.

The sheriff spoke to his deputy. "James, go get the coroner and bring him here." He turned back to Jack. "I'll need you to sign the affidavit on what happened and then I'll get a couple of these men to witness it. Don't leave until I get back." Jack nodded saying he would wait and went to the bar with Leslie to get that drink…or two.

The sheriff looked at the horses tied to the rail outside the bar. Men out here paid attention to the horses other men rode and could identify them as well as they could the men who rode them. He looked at the brand on the only horse he did not recognize and wasn't surprised to see the 'lazy A' brand on its flank. He walked quickly to his office to read the telegram again describing the robber and killer of a bank teller and a rancher by the name of Anderson in San Antonio. The description was one describing the wanted man as six feet tall, well built, blue eyes and long blonde hair.

"Damn!" He mumbled. He checked his Colt and taking a shotgun off the rack behind his desk took a deep breath and headed back to the saloon to arrest the killer.

Walking into the saloon he saw the man calling himself Ben Wilkerson standing at the bar with Leslie Holcomb, the local cowboy who was happy to be alive. The two men stood with their backs to the door and the sheriff.

"Jack Gillespie," the sheriff said loudly and saw the man calling himself Ben back stiffen. "I'm arresting you for murder."

Leslie turned and said, "Sheriff you heard what I said as well as everyone else in here. What's going on?"

"I'm arresting him for the murder of a rancher in San Antonio by the name of Anderson and a young bank teller he shot during a robbery a few days ago." He cocked the hammers on the twin barreled scattergun. "Drop your gun Jack." Jack was looking at the sheriff in the mirror behind the bar. He slowly turned around and faced the lawman.

"My names Ben Wilkerson sheriff. You must be mistaken," he said smiling speaking with a warm southern twang to his voice.

"Maybe, maybe not," the sheriff answered. "Just drop your gun and we'll talk about it."

Jack had begun unbuckling his gun belt not wanting to argue with a man holding a scattergun pointed at his belly when a glass was accidently knocked off a table by one the bystanders watching the drama. The saloon was as quiet as a Church and when the glass shattered the noise was extremely loud. The sheriff's eyes turned toward the noise for just an instant and Jack took advantage of the situation. With his left hand he jerked a startled Leslie in front of him and at the same time drew his own Colt. The shotgun's explosion shattered the quietness followed by two quick blasts from Jack's Colt. Two bloody spots appeared on the front of the lawman's shirt and he staggered backwards before crumpling to the floor. Jack still held the lifeless body of Leslie who had taken the full load of buckshot in the chest. Holding Leslie's dead body as a shield he turned the gun on the patrons' of the saloon.

"The first bastard that moves is dead," he spat out, his voice stern, mo longer showing the southern charm. He dropped Leslie and reached down and took the cowboys Colt from its leather then moved toward the door. "Anyone sticks his damn head out that door will lose it," he warned.

"There's a lot of us mister," one of the men said standing a few feet in front of Jack, "and only one of you." Jack looked at the blue clad soldier doing the talking and pulled the trigger on the pistol. The soldier fell to his knees, clutching the hole in his belly with both hands, a startled look on his face. The soldier stayed in that position for a couple of seconds and pitched forward dead before he hit the floor.

"Anyone else got anything to say?" Dead silence followed the question. Backing out the door he turned and saw the sheriff's deputy running toward the saloon from across the street. Jack feathered the trigger of his Colt and the slug took the deputy in the chest stopping him in his tracks. He stuck his Colt in his holster and shifting the gun he had picked up from his left to his right hand jerked the reins of his horse from the rail and jumping into the saddle, fired a shot for good measure into the bat winged door of the saloon. *That should keep the bastards heads down for a few seconds,* he mused. No one fired at him from any of the buildings as he rode out of town because they didn't know what had happened or who the man was riding hell bent for leather out of their town.

Jack slowed his horse to a gallop and pondered on what he would do next. He was glad the poles along the road that were put up for the new telegraph had no wire up yet. *That's the only good luck I've had lately*, he thought. Reining his mount to a trot and then a walk to let him get his wind back for the run he was sure was coming when the posse showed up behind him.

~~

Back in Uvalde it had taken thirty minutes to get a posse together. They rode out in pursuit of the killer promising themselves they would get the son-of-a-bitch and hang him. Like most posses though they were mostly married men and men who had businesses to run. They had not taken the time to gather supplies or water in their haste so by not catching up to the outlaw by dark, turned their mounts back toward Uvalde and their families.

~~

Jack lay down on his bed in the bunkhouse. He felt the uneasiness of the other two men there knowing they knew who he was since one of them had told Jarrod about a Jack Gillespie who was a cold-blooded killer. He would stay and rest up for another day or so and then go on to Mexico. He would love to stay and become a partner with his brother, but sooner or later his past would catch up to him and he didn't want to bring trouble here, to his brother and his family. For the first time he felt a twinge of regret for the path he had taken.

Chapter Fourteen

Tye sat on Sandy in front of a small, but well kept ranch house waiting for someone to come to the door after he had hollered "Hello the house." It would be considered unmannerly to dismount and walk to the door without being asked. Besides, just walking up to mans door without an invite might just get you shot.

The door opened and a middle aged woman stepped out holding a double barreled shotgun. Tye smiled. *These people aren't pilgrims. I bet they have seen trouble and know how to take care of it.* Tye tipped his hat to the lady. She was a large woman, not fat but big boned and probably an inch or two under six foot. She wore a man's plaid shirt and brown pants. Tye had no doubt that she knew how to handle the shotgun and would use it if she had to.

"Good morning. I was passing through and thought I might ask you a few questions about a fellow I'm trying to locate."

"Aren't you Tye Watkins, the scout at Clark?" Tye, set back some by her knowing him smiled and answered.

"Yes, I was a scout but now I'm a deputy U.S. Marshall." He paused for a couple of seconds. "How did you know my name.?"

The woman lowered the scatter-gun. "Step down and come in and have a cup of coffee." Tye was impressed by the inside of the house and how neat and clean it was. The furniture was all handmade, built by a man who was damn good with his hands.

"Nice place you have here Mrs...."

"Daniels...Lucy Daniels. My husband is Bill Daniels." She motioned to a chair at the table. Tye sat down as she was placing a steaming cup of coffee in front of him.

"Your husband make this furniture?"

She nodded. "Bill has a knack for building things." She laughed. "He's a better carpenter than a farmer. We'd starve if it wasn't for his making and selling things to the neighbors around here. He's a good man though; honest as the day is long, hard worker, and loves me and the kids. What else could a woman need.?"

Tye placed the cup down after taking a sip. "That's all any man or woman could ask of his mate. You didn't say how you knew me?"

We were in Brackett about a year and a half ago with some neighbors of ours who had their daughter stolen by the Apaches. We were there when you came in after killing that terrible Apache, Tanza, and brought in those captive children. The little girl was our neighbors daughter they thought was dead. That was one of the best days of my life seeing the happiness you brought to that family; one that I will remember forever. Thank you.

Tye remembered that day also and that bastard Tanza who had killed his best friends the Turley's and taken their grandkids captive. Two of those children he brought back were them. They had been taken in and were being raised by Master Sergeant O'Malley and his wife. It was a bitter taste in his mouth remembering. Tanza and his followers killed a lot of people before he was killed.

"What brings you up here?"

"Looking for a ranch owned by a fellow named Gillespie."

She looked startled. "Why, are you going to arrest him for something? They are such good neighbors and are wonderful people on top of that. Why in the world is the law after him?"

Tye chuckled. "I'm not after him Mrs. Daniels. I'm looking for his brother, Jack."

"Thank goodness. I just couldn't imagine Jarrod Gillespie doing anything against the law." She looked down at her hands then back at Tye. "His brother have blue eyes and blonde hair?"

Tye nodded. "You've seen him then?"

Three days, maybe four ago, this man came by looking for a ranch owned by a man named Gillespie. I figured he was an out of work cowboy and never gave it a second thought-until now. Why are you looking for him?"

He's bad though and through Mrs. Daniels. He killed a woman in a saloon in Fort Worth, killed a man in Houston, killed a sheriff and deputy along with a soldier in Uvalde and most recently killed another soldier and wounded a lieutenant in Brackett."

"My God. And you know for a fact this man's brother is Jarrod Gillespie."

"I only know his brother reportably has a ranch somewhere up here and since you described him a few minutes ago, I figure it to be true." Tye sat his coffee cup down. "Do you know where this ranch is?"

"Yes. Bill and I have been there a few times and Jarrod and Martha, that's Jarrod's wife, have been here a few times. Their ranch is two miles west of Old Fort Terrett which is just a few miles farther north of here."

Tye downed the last of his coffee and stood up. "I've never been there, but I can find it. He picked up his hat from the back of the chair. "I want to thank you for your hospitality and for the information. Tell your husband what I said about his handiwork and maybe I'll see you again." He turned and walked out the door. After the coolness of the house the air outside felt like a furnace. He mounted Sandy and tipped his hat again to Mrs. Daniels who was standing on the porch with her raised hand shielding her eyes from the glare of the sun.

"You be careful Mr. Watkins. We need men like you out here." She smiled and added. "Alive that is."

Tye laughed. "I intend to stay that way Mrs. Daniels." Good day and thanks again." He reined Sandy around and headed north at an easy gallop. Lucy Daniels stood on the porch watching him until he disappeared over the crest of the nearby hill. *I can't wait to tell Bill about Tye being here-and in our house.* Then she thought of why he was here. *I do hope that it's not true about that terrible man being Jarrod's brother.* She walked to the side of the house and pulled the ax from the log it was stuck in and began chopping some kindling for the stove.

Tye reached Fort Terrett, or what use to be a fort, an hour later. Terrett was established in 1852 to protect the settlers in the area. He knew it had been named for a Lieutenant Terrett that had been killed a few years before it was established. He didn't know any details as to why it was abandoned in 1854. He led Sandy over to a circular rock wall he figured to be a well. He could see an old wooden bucket with a rope attached on top of the wall. He was pleasantly surprised when he dropped the bucket into the darkness of the well to hear it splash when it hit water.

After his and Sandy's drinking their fill of the cold water he filled his canteens, placed the bucket back on top of the wall for the next traveler to find and spent a few minutes looking around the abandoned old fort. Surprised the old fort had been so well built with several stone buildings he made a mental note to find out why it had been abandoned. He mounted Sandy and reined him around and headed west to find the Gillespie ranch.

Jack Gillespie had spent the whole day rounding up strays and herding them to a temporary corral he and the other two cowboys had built to hold them till they could be branded. All day he had this nagging feeling he should leave because trouble was headed his way and he didn't want his brother and his family involved. He walked over to Bill, one of the cowboys.

"Bill, I know you and Lester know about my past." He waited a second before continuing seeing Bill's surprise at his words. "I don't want to bring trouble to this ranch and my brother, but I got a gut feeling it's headed this way. Tell Jarrod that I will write to him when I get to where I'm going-wherever that is. He mounted his horse. "Been a pleasure knowing you Bill. Tell Lester the same." He tipped his hat and turned his horse and headed west at an easy gallop leaving Bill standing there wondering what the hell all that was about. He had grown to like Jack and really wondered if all the stories about him were true or not. He figured some were because Jack had just admitted about things in his past, but he also knew how news traveling by word of mouth out here could be a lot different after several telling it than what it was originally was.

Jack rode west toward Mexico with all his worldly belongings in his saddlebags: two extra shirts, a pair of pants and extra underwear in one bag. In the other he had some food which consisted of dried jerky and some sourdough biscuits and extra ammunition. His slicker was tied behind his saddle with his bedroll. *Not much to show for a man my age,* he mused. *Got no home, no woman and no kids. Just got what I have on, my horse and what's in those bags.* He reined his mount back to a trot and then a walk. He pushed the brim of his hat up and looked back over his shoulder. *No one depending on me either and no one to answer to and I've got two thousand dollars right here,* he thought as he patted his shirt pocket. *That's more than any cowboy has working his ass off for some damn rich rancher.* His slight feeling of remorse of the things he had done were only fleeting thoughts as he now focused on what he was going to do with greenbacks stuffed in his pocket-women and liquor and more women. He chuckled.

Chapter Fifteen

Tye, sitting on Sandy on a rocky knoll, looked down at the ranch house he figured was the Gillespie's about a quarter mile away. The sun was dropping below the horizon so he decided to make camp and ride in to the ranch early in the morning while the hands would be eating breakfast and not scattered all over range. If there was gunplay he wanted it in full daylight, not in the dark. He had seen no signs of any springs or water holes so his would be a dry camp. He back tracked about another quarter of mile so no one would accidently stumble into his camp and picketed Sandy in a patch of grama grass. He pitched his bedroll nearby and sat down with some dried jerky and a biscuit washing it down with some of the warm water in his canteen.

By the time he finished his meal it was full dark. Taking off his gun belt and removing his Bowie from his boot, he lay down on the bedroll and placed the weapons beside him within easy reach. His Henry was also within reach propped up against a juniper.

Lying on his back looking up at the night sky he thought of Rebecca and the kids and how much he missed them. He also thought of the troops at Clark and the many friends he had there and wondered if anything was going on with them and the Apache.

Hell, he mused, *I even miss them, the Apache.* His thoughts drifted back to the many friends he had lost the last two or so years, both white and Apache. He remembered the Turley's who had been killed along with their son and daughter-in-law and their two children who had been taken captive by the Apaches on a raid on their homestead two years ago. He had tracked down the Apaches and rescued the Turley children along with two other captives. He had know the Turley family all his life since they had been neighbors to his family and after his ma and pa's death had almost been like second parents to him and helped him so much.

He thought of Lieutenant Garrison that had been killed only a short time ago and of Sergeant Christian whom he had been on many patrols with who was killed only two months ago. He wondered about the men he had recently captured Cole Frazier and his brothers and if they were at the fort or had been sent to Fort Inge or back to San Antonio. Men like the Frazier's were the type of men he despised; men too lazy to work and preyed on those that did. He respected the Apache and fully understood why they fought against the white man. He had no feeling of hate for them even though his father and many friends had been killed by them. If he had been born Apache, he would be doing the same.

He lay there pondering these things until the stars appeared above him. As usual when on camp like this, he located the different constellations his pa had showed him years before. He thought of his parents and how much they had meant to him. Living where they did they didn't have a lot of material things, but they had shared a lot of love. The two worse days of his life had been when he had to bury them. "God, I miss them so much," he mumbled out loud. Sandy quit munching the grass and looking at his master, nickered softly. Tye looked at his horse, his friend, smiled and went to sleep.

At Fort Clark, Major Thurston had his hands full. The people in Brackett wanted to hang the Frazier's, but so did the commanding officer at Fort Inge as well as the law in San Antonio. *Hell, I want to hang the bastards myself,* he thought as he sat at his desk. Two families had come into the fort earlier with one dead family member and two others wounded by Apaches at their homesteads located southwest of the fort. Master Sergeant O'Malley had reported two soldiers had apparently deserted during the previous night since they were not present at reveille this morning. He had dispatched a scout and four soldiers to find them and bring them back-alive if possible.

Desertion was a problem all the forts had along the border and Thurston understood why. Loneliness, heat, boredom, Apaches, not much money a month-if they got paid at all wore heavy on a man. He understood these things because when he was young he had the same thoughts about army life himself. He understood the reasons, but he could not condone it. When they did desert they took government weapons and government horses with them. That made them thieves as well as deserters and he would punish them as such.

He had sent his best scout, Dan August, and a patrol to the homesteads of the families who came in earlier to see if they could pick up the tracks of the raiders. The homesteads were near the border and both Thurston and Dan knew the Apaches already had probably headed back into the safety of Mexico. *One of these days, I'm going to say to hell with politics and chase them down in Mexico and put an end to their raiding over here and then crossing back into Mexico knowing we will not follow.* He thought about it and chuckled, *It would probably be the end of my career though.* He stood up and after stretching the kinks out of his body headed to his quarters. "It's been one hell of a day," He mumbled out loud."

"His orderly stood up quickly when Thurston came out of his office. "Did you say something Sir?"

Thurston smiled at the corporal. "Nothing important-nothing at all. I will see you in the morning."

After a restless night trying to sleep on the unusually uneven and rocky ground, Tye approached the ranch house at first light not in the best of moods. As he entered the yard a man came out of the main house. He was obviously startled to see Tye sitting on Sandy in his yard.

"Who are you?" the man asked in a booming voice that showed both authority and maybe just a hint of uneasiness since he was caught outside without his gun on his hip. His voice carried into the bunkhouse where the men were eating breakfast and the cook and the two hands, Bill and Lester, stepped out their plates in one hand and their Colts in the other.

Tye, knowing the distrust people had of strangers sat there with his palms on the pommel of his saddle making no sudden moves.

"Is this the Gillespie ranch?"

The man who came out of the main house answered, "It is."

"Name is Tye Watkins from down Fort Clark ways."

"You the scout everyone has heard of?"

Tye nodded. "Sure would fill a mite more comfortable if those men would holster those six shooters."

The man smiled and looking at his men said, "It's okay." He watched as they holstered their guns and went back inside to finish eating. Jarrod walked over to Tye. "Step down and have some breakfast." As Tye stepped down the man took Sandy's reins and looped them over the rail and then stuck out his hand. "My name's Jarrod

Gillespie and this is my place," he said shaking hands with Tye.

Tye had already seen that the place had been well built and kept in top shape. "Nice place," he said following Jarrod into the bunkhouse. The ranch did not have a separate kitchen and dining area so one end of the bunkhouse was being used as of now.

Jarrod introduced Tye to the cook, Bill and Lester.

"Heard you've fought an Apache or two," Bill said.

Tye smiled. "I've had an encounter or two before."

Jarrod chuckled. "From what I've heard that is one of the biggest understatements I have ever heard."

Tye laughed along with the other men. "I was on the Apaches most 'wanted' list for a long time."

"What do you mean by...was?" Jarrod asked.

"I retired from chasing Apaches a month or so ago. I'm a deputy U.S. Marshall now." Jarrod and the other men's mood darkened immediately. The cook went to washing dishes and Bill and Lester excused themselves saying they needed to get to work.

Not really wanting to ask, but he had to anyway Jarrod spoke. "What brings you all the way up here?"

Tye, knowing that his brother was here or at least was here was a little on the defensive now and carefully chose his words.

"There was a shooting in Uvalde a few days ago and most recently, in Brackett. Men were killed and wounded some being soldiers and others were law officers. This followed some killings and a robbery in San Antonio and Houston."

"What's this have to do with me?"

"Nothing with you Jarrod, but maybe your brother Jack. He was identified by people in Houston and the description they gave fits the man who shot up Uvalde and Brackett."

"My brother is not a damn killer," Jarrod blurted out.

Tye smiled trying to keep a lid on things. "You may be right Jarrod. It might not be your brother, but I need to talk to him and ask a few questions."

"How can you come in here and accept my hospitality and then say my brother is a damn murderer and robber? Jarrod said obviously becoming very defensive and agitated.

"Look Mr. Gillespie. I don't know if your brother is guilty of these things or not. That is for a jury to decide. I just want to talk with him and hear his side of the story, if he is the one involved. I know that circumstances sometimes cause men to do things they would not normally do and then things snowball after that. I've known men, good men that sometimes trouble just follows them, hanging over them like a storm cloud over the mountains and won't go away. It would be better to face things and get them worked out than to let things fester. There is a bounty on his head and there will be men after him that won't give a damn if they bring him in dead or alive."

Jarrod sighed and leaned back in his chair. "He's not here Tye. He left yesterday telling Bill he didn't want to bring trouble down on me and the ranch."

"Where did he go?"

"He told Bill he was headed west to Mexico."

Tye stood up. "Can you show me where Bill last saw him?"

"I don't know for sure. Bill should be a mile west of here working some breaks looking for cattle." He took a pen and paper from his pocket and scribbled a note. "Give this to Bill." He shook Tye's hand. "Try to bring him in alive Tye. Maybe he's done those things, but he's the only kin I got left."

"I'll do that Jarrod. You can count on it."Tye mounted Sandy and rode out of the yard toward where Jarrod said Bill should be.

A short time later he found Bill with a rope around an old mossy-back trying to pull him out of some brush that the steer didn't want to come out of. Tye took his rope and deftly threw it at the steer and it looped around the steer horns which were more than five and a half foot from tip to tip. Looping the rope around the saddle horn he backed Sandy up. The old longhorn was strong but couldn't hold back with two horses pulling on him.

"Thanks Tye," Bill said wiping the sweat from him his face with his kerchief. "Been wrestling with that old mossback for almost an hour and just about ready to give up. That's one old steer you don't want to be on the ground around cause he's sure as hell would try and get you with those horns" He removed Tye's rope from the steers horns. "You looking for me?"

Tye nodded as he coiled the rope and tied it to the piece of rawhide on his saddle. "Jarrod said you might be able to show me where you last saw Jack." He handed the note to Bill.

Bill unfolded the piece of paper and looked at the message.

Bill-show the marshal where you last saw Jack so he can pick up his trail. I think Watkins will try and bring him back alive and others won't.

Jarrod

Bill folded the note back up and looked at Tye. "Let's go." He reined his horse around and headed east. They trotted their mounts for about ten minutes before Bill held up. "We talked over there," he said nodding to a thick stand of juniper and cedar. "He headed west. "He said he figured trouble was coming and he didn't want to bring it here to the ranch." Bill looked off in the distance toward where he watched Jack ride away. "You know something Marshal, he might have done a lot of bad things, but I liked him. He was a good worker and fun to be around. It just don't figure out him being a killer."

"Knew a man once," Tye said, "That was the friendless, kindest, most honest man you could find until he started drinking and then he was short tempered, foul mouthed, and would shoot you at the drop of a hat. I knew another that was a good guy, but everywhere he went trouble followed him. A little trouble at first then it snowballed on him and things just kept getting worse. I think Jack is like the latter, basically a good guy that's had a lot of things go against him and he's had to do some bad

177

things to survive. I hope to find him and bring him back without a fight, but with what's happened every time the law closes in," he looked away and sighed, "I don't think he will come in peaceable like."

Bill reached over and stuck out his hand which Tye took. "I know you will try Marshal. Good luck." He rode back toward where that old ornery steer was left.

Tye picked up Jacks trail and dismounted to study the horses tracks so he would recognize them if they intermingled with other tracks later. Every horse has a particular way of walking that is different from another horse and sometimes it is easy to pick out the track you are looking for because of a notch in a shoe. Jack's horse left front hoof turned in slightly. Satisfied he could stay on this horses trail he mounted Sandy, leaned forward and scratched him on the neck.

"We got us some serious riding to do Sandy. This here cowboy has an eleven or twelve hour head start and I'm betting he ain't going to let any moss grow under his horses hooves. You ready ole boy?" He smiled when Sandy nickered and nodded his head. "Let's go then," he said giving Sandy a slight nudge in the flanks with his heels.

Chapter Sixteen

Jack had ridden last night until darkness closed in around him. He made a cold camp eating cold biscuits, a little jerky and washing it down with water from his canteen. He gave his horse a little more water than he had drank knowing he would probably die out here if his ride gave out on him.

He had broke camp that morning a little before daylight. Two hours later he came across some tracks of about ten or so horses. The tracks were fresh, probably no more than an hour or so old and a cold chill eased its way up Jacks spine. The tracks were unshod-Indian ponies. He stood up and studied the terrain all around him. Seeing nothing he remounted and continued west, but at a much slower pace. He wanted to raise no dust nor make any more noise than necessary. He rode with his Henry across his thighs and his eyes moving in every direction, alert for any sign of trouble.

He rode the rest of the day this way stopping only to give his horse a blow every couple hours. He chewed jerky and drank a little water while in the saddle. His canteen was less than half full now so not only the Indians were a worry, but water also. An hour before dusk he found what he figured was the Rio Pecos River. Here was water, but getting to it was going to be a problem. High cliffs were as far as he could see up and down the river. He had dismounted and standing on the cliff over the river the water must have been sixty or more feet below him. Knowing the Pecos would eventually run into the Rio Grande he headed south, down river.

~~

Earlier, Tye had come to where Jack's horse's tracks crossed the unshod tracks of several horses. Stepping from the saddle he pulled his Henry from its saddle scabbard and before studying the tracks up close he looked at the terrain around him in all directions at every rock, bush, and any other place that might hide trouble. Satisfied he was alone he dropped to one knee for a closer look at the tracks. After looking at how much the sand had filled the tracks and poking a pile of horse dung with a stick he estimated the Indians were there about five or six hours earlier and Jack had been there shortly thereafter. He saw where Jack's horses tracks left the torn up ground of the Indian's pony's hooves.

Standing beside Sandy he looked in the direction Jack was headed and muttered out loud. "He's making a bee line for Mexico for sure old buddy. The only problem I see is that where he is headed there's no place to cross the Rio Grande." He slipped the toe of his boot in the stirrup and stepped easily into the saddle. He sat there for a long moment thinking about what Jack would do when he found out he can't cross the river where he is because of the cliffs. *He'll have to go north or south,* Tye mused. *He wants to get to Mexico so I'm guessing south. I'll follow his tracks for about twenty or so miles then angle south to where the nearest crossing is.* He nudged Sandy to trot following Jack's tracks.

He had gone about five miles when he pulled Sandy up sharply. "Damn," he said loudly. "Damn and double damn," he repeated. Looking at the ground he saw four separate tracks of unshod ponies and they had been made less than an hour earlier. He leaned down from the saddle and saw moccasin tracks where one of the Indians had dismounted and studied the tracks of Jacks' horse. Not going to miss the chance of finding a lone white man they were on his trail. There was no problem following five sets of tracks so Tye kicked Sandy into a gallop hoping to close the gap between the Indians, Jack and himself.

He alternated galloping, trotting and walking Sandy for the next two hours and now was giving the big horse a rest and letting him drink from a seep he found in a rock wall. He jerked his head up when he heard what sounded like several shots fired close together. He pulled Sandy's head from the seep and headed in the direction of the shots. "Jacks found himself some Apaches, "he said leaning forward and low in the saddle patting Sandy on the neck as they rushed toward the sound of the guns. He reined in when it sounded like he was close to the fight. Only sporadic firing could be heard now. As he inched his way up the slope of the hill he heard the distinctive 'Boom' of a big fifty. " On his belly and taking his hat off he snuck a quick peek over the crest of the hill. It was a quick look not wanting to show himself any longer than necessary. With that quick look he saw Jack was in big time trouble. His horse was down and apparently dead. Jack was in a jumble of big rocks and in a pretty good defensive position but Tye bet his food was still in the saddle bags and canteen on his saddle. Tye took another look and saw that indeed his bags was still on the dead horse and figured his canteen was too. It didn't surprise Tye that was the case. Tye shook his head. He knew most men in a situation of being chased by Apaches think of finding a place to hole up first and then think of food and water later when they can't get to them. Jack's horse was laying only ten or so feet from where Jack was hidden but the time it would take to get to them would allow several shots to be fired at him from his attackers.

Tye eased his head over the rocks again and ducked quickly as he saw a puff of smoke flowed by the boom of the 'fifty'. He heard the sound of the heavy lead splitting the air as it passed over where his head had been an instant earlier. He shook his head and swallowed. *That was close,* he thought. *The Apache must have seen me earlier and was waiting for me to raise my head again.* He slid back down the slope a few feet and then in a crouch, ran about twenty yards to his right. He bellied up the slope again and found himself behind some thick cedars. With his rifle barrel slowly pushed some foliage to the side and peered through the opening. He could see two of the Apaches plainly and one of them high on the slope was the one that had fired at him with the Sharps.

He took his kerchief off and wiped the sweat from his eyes and forehead. The Apache was only fifty yards away and Tye had a good angle that should be an easy shot. He levered a shell into the chamber after waiting for shots to be fired to cover the sound of the shell being injected into the chamber. He was far enough away that he figured they could not hear it anyway, but he didn't want to chance it. His only chance was to kill the brave with the Sharps and then the one right below him which would cut the odds down to even-two versus two.

Sighting in on the Sharps carrying Apache, Tye placed his sight on the head, just above the ear. He took a deep breath and then slowly exhaled and feathered the trigger. The butt of his Henry slammed into his shoulder as it spit out the forty-four cal. slug. Tye was swinging the barrel at the other Apache as the lead from the Henry exploded the Apaches head that held the 'big fifty'. Tye squeezed the trigger of his Henry a second time and saw a red hole on the second Apache as the lead put a hole in the warriors chest and exploded out the his back. The force of the forty-four knocked him down the slope toward where Jack lay in the rocks.

"What the hell?" Jack exclaimed as he saw two of his attackers tumbled down the slopes. As he was wondering what had happened the other two remaining warriors made a dash for their horses. Jack raised his Henry and fired three shots as fast as he could lever the trigger, but hit no one. Three seconds later he heard the sound of running horses. He stood up and walked to where his horse lay and laying his rifle down and picked up his canteen and lifted it to his lips. As he took a deep drink his eyes lifted to the slope in front on him and he saw a white man making his way down the slope. He knew this was the man who saved his life and he took another swallow watching him closely. It was a big man he was watching and he moved easily down the slippery slope. He carried the rifle in his left hand, his right not far from the butt of his pistol on his right hip. He was within twenty feet when Jack realized his rifle lay across his dead horse. He lifted his pistol a couple inches from his holster to make sure it had not become jammed down in it during his scramble from his horse to the rocks. It came out loose and easy so he dropped it back in. He wanted to meet this man and find out why he was out here in the middle of nowhere and why he risked his life to save him.

Tye stopped when he hit level ground about ten feet from where the outlaw stood.

"You alright?" he asked.

Jack hesitated just a second sizing the man up. He saw a man who was big, over six foot and thick through the shoulders. He carried a big Bowie in his right boot, a pistol on his hip and carried the Henry in his left hand. He also noticed the grip was just above the lever and his finger was on the trigger. All the man had to do was raise the barrel and pull the trigger. He could tell immediately this man was a dangerous man, one who was accustomed to violence and there was no doubt in his mind that if he made the wrong move he was a dead man. "I'm fine," he said, "Which is more than I can say for my horse," he added nodding to where the animal lay. "Lucky for me you happen to come along when you did. What's your name if you don't mind me asking?"

"Tye Watkins."

Jack looked a little startled. "You the scout from Fort Clark?"

Tye nodded. "Was. Not anymore."

"You quit?"

"Took another job. A job I figured was a little safer than chasing Apaches."

"Hell man, any job would be safer than that," Jack said smiling. "What are you doing now for a living?"

"Took a job as a U.S. Marshall." Tye saw the man stiffen.

"What are you doing out here in the middle of nowhere?" Jack asked his eyes shifting to where his rifle lay and back at Tye.

"Looking for you if you're Jack Gillespie."

The man chuckled. "Well you saved the wrong man. My name is George Rogers."

"Don't think so," Tye said. "I've followed the tracks of that horse lying there all the way from your brother's ranch. You also fit the description I have." Tye saw the look of desperation in the man's eyes and watched as the outlaws hand move a couple inches closer to the Colt on his hip. "Don't try for the gun Jack," Tye said as he raised the barrel of his Henry a few inches to where it was pointing at Jack's chest. "There's a reward for you Jack and there will be a lot of bounty hunters that don't give a damn whether they bring you in dead or alive. I promised your brother I would bring you in alive if at all possible so unbuckle the gun belt and let it fall to the ground."

Jack waited a couple of seconds weighing his chances of drawing his gun before the lawman could pull the trigger. He knew he was fast himself, but the man holding the gun on him had a long standing reputation as a fighting man. He reached slowly with his left hand and unbuckled his belt. As it slipped from his hips he dropped his right hand and drew the Colt from the falling holster. The movement was a faster than the eye could follow, but Tye's reflexes honed from years of fighting Apaches were quicker. He feathered the trigger on the Henry and moved to the left at the same time. A bullet burned the air where his head had been an instant earlier. Jack had drew and fired just as the forty-four slug hit him high in the left chest spinning him around almost knocking him to the ground. He was hit hard but he raised his Colt again and thumbed the hammer back on the single action Colt.

"Don't do it Jack," Tye hollered. "Drop it." Jack brought the barrel up and Tye squeezed the trigger again and the rifle belched another slug of lead. Tye saw a puff of dust on Jacks shirt as the bullet hit him in the chest and an instant later exploded out his back in a spray of blood. The solid hit from that close of range lifted Jack off his feet and backwards a couple of steps before he hit the ground hard. Tye was over him in a second, kicking the Colt away from the man's hand.

"Dammit Jack, I told you not to try it."

"H…had to Ma…Marshal. Ha…had…," He closed his eyes and coughed as a large amount of frothy blood ran from the corner of his mouth. He opened his eyes as he struggled to speak. "Di…didn't wa..want to go to prison or han…" He didn't finish as he took a deep breath, exhaled slowly and died.

Tye stood slowly up and looked down at the body of the man with the name of Bloody Jack and shook his head. He climbed back up the slope to get Sandy. Returning, he rounded up one of the Indian ponies and after a struggle, got Jack's saddle off the dead horse and on the Indian pony. He lifted the outlaw's body and gently laid it across the saddle. He tied his hands with a rope and drew the end under the belly of the pony and tied it to Jacks feet pulling it tight to hold him in the saddle. He picked up Jack's Colt and Henry placing the rifle in the boot on the outlaw's saddle and the Colt in one of his saddle bags. He stepped back and looking at Jack shook his head. *What a waste,* he thought. *Good looking kid and probably smart enough to have figured out a way to make a honest living and raise a family.*

Afraid the Apaches would be back with some friends he left at an easy gallop glancing back often to make sure Jack's body was still in the saddle. He also was checking for trouble following him. He held the horses to a gallop for several minutes then to a walk and then back to a gallop. He repeated this time and again for the next few hours stopping only twice to give Sandy and the Indian pony a breather and some water.   As dark was setting in he found a steep hill that had some boulders scattered about on the top which would offer some protection for him and the horses. It took him several minutes leading both horses up the slope that was covered in loose rocks and sand. Exhausted, he sat down and looking back to the west for any signs of Apaches, he watched the sun dip below the horizon and dusk turned to night.

He had no intention of spending the night here figuring on staying only long enough to give the horses a good rest and when the moon was out to give off a little light he would be moving again. The feeling in his gut told him trouble wasn't far behind and his gut wasn't wrong often. His gut also reminded him he hadn't put anything in it for quite a spell. He walked over to where Sandy was picketed nibbling on the short grama grass. Reaching into his saddlebag he took out a good size chunk of jerky, took his canteen that was looped around the pommel his saddle, sat on a rock and chewed the jerky watching and listening for any hint of visitors. He was tired and needed some sleep, but knowing Apaches the way he did he knew better. He just sat, watching and listeneing.

Looking at the stars and judging it to be about midnight he led the horses down the slope and toeing the stirrup with his left boot swung his right leg over the saddle and headed east still wondering where the Apaches were. He took care in trying to make it difficult as possible for the Apaches to follow him. When possible he stayed on rocky ground and once stayed in a small stream for a half mile before exiting and continuing east. He knew the warriors would not lose his trail but he could slow them down some and not make it easy.

As the sun was breaking the horizon in front of him he looked at the terrain and saw several things that told him he was just west of the Gillespie ranch, maybe three or four miles. He figured he had made it, but as usual out here in this part of Texas you can never take anything for granted, when he heard the report of a rifle and several angry shrieks of the Apaches coming up fast behind him.

He pulled his Henry from its boot and slapped the Indian pony on the rump to get it going and nudged Sandy into a fast gallop. He glanced over his shoulder and saw five Apaches no more than a hundred and fifty yards behind him. Tye knew he could not outrun the Apache ponies because the one he led was holding him back. His only chance was to get close enough that the ranch hands could hear the rifle shots.

He had run maybe a mile when he glanced over his shoulder. The Apaches had closed to about a hundred yards and he could almost see their smiles of victory. The race would not have been close if Sandy could run full out. Glancing about he recognized the high cliff wall that was chalk white, the one he had seen just after speaking with the ranch hand named Bill who had showed him Jack's tracks headed west. He was only a mile from the ranch house. He started to glance over his shoulder when a piece of hot lead burned the air by his right ear. He leaned forward to where his chest was almost touching the Pommel of his saddle. He didn't want to lead the Apaches to the Gillespie's door step so he was looking for a defensive position to try and hold them off till the ranch hands showed up. He figured he was close enough for them to hear the rifles and he would also fire his Colt which was louder than the crack of the Henry's to get their attention.

He was still looking when rifle fire broke out just in front of him. He glanced over his shoulder just in time to see one warrior tumble off the back of his racing pony and another grab his shoulder and slumped in the saddle. The

Apaches tuned their mounts around and after picking up their dead brother and not knowing how many whites they had stumbled onto headed back the way they had come.

Tye slowed his horses to a walk then stopped as he saw Bill and the other ranch hand walking their horses from some thick cedars.

"Looks like you could use some help Marshal," Bill said with a big grin on his face which quickly faded when he recognized the body of Jack.

Tye saw the expression on the man's face change. He quickly spoke up. "He didn't give me no choice Bill. I found him fighting off these Apaches. I stepped in sorter like you did just now and surprised them. I got the drop on Jack and told him to unbuckle his gun belt which he did. The only problem was as it was dropping to the ground he pulled his pistol out so fast it was just a blur. His bullet just missed my head. I had my Henry on him when he drew and I'm more than a fair shot. Before he thumbed back the hammer for another try at me I shot him in the shoulder. I didn't want to kill him Bill, understand that. Mainly because that's what I promised your boss I would do. When he raised the Colt the second time I had no choice but to kill him."

Bill looked straight at Tye then at Jack and shrugged his shoulder. I'm sure that's the way it happened. You could have lied and said the Apaches killed him and no one would have been the wiser."

"I would have known Bill. I couldn't live with that. By the way, how did you two happen to be out here?"

"We were just over the hill there," he said nodding to his right, "When we heard the shooting. Came to investigate and saved the life of a famous scout and marshal."

"Well, I sure have to agree with that," Tye said smiling.

"Let's get Jack to the Ranch," Bill said taking the reins of the Indian pony from Tye.

Jarrod Gillespie was in the yard of his ranch house with a rifle waiting to see what all the shooting was about. Tye saw the rifle drop from the ranchers hand when he recognized the body draped over the Indian pony. He rushed to the body and raised the head up to verify it was his brother.

Sobbing, he looked up at Tye. "You said you would bring him in alive." He reached for his pistol. Tye kicked Sandy in the flank and the surprised horse jumped forward hitting the rancher hard and knocking him to the ground.

Tye was off Sandy before the man quit rolling and quickly walked to him and kicked the gun from his hand before the man could get his senses back. Tye kneeled and put his hand under the stunned man's back and raised him to a sitting position. He waited till the man's eyes could focus and then raised him to his feet and dusted off Jarrod's clothes.

He quickly related what happened that resulted him killing Jack. "His last words were that he did not want to go to prison or hang. I brought him here because I thought you would want to be the one to bury him."

Jarrod nodded his head. "I apologize for my actions a minute ago. I don't know what came over me."

"No apology necessary Jarrod. I understand." Tye answered picking up Jarrod's gun and sticking it in the grieving man's holster.

"I'm sure that's the way it was." Jarrod said. " Jack told me he had done some things he was ashamed of and that trouble seemed to just follow him everywhere he went." He wiped his hands on his pants and stuck his right hand out to shake Tye's hand. Tye took it and they shook holding the shake for a moment. Jarrod said. "I appreciate you bringing him back Marshal. I know you didn't have to.

You could have ridden back to Clark and I would have never known what happened to my brother."

"If it had been my brother I would have wanted to know. That's why I brought him back."

Jarrod's wife came to where they were standing. She had been in the doorway and heard everything. "We appreciate you doing this Tye. You're a good man just like we had heard."

Tye tipped his hat to the lady. "There are a few men who might argue that point." He toed the stirrup of his saddle and swung into the saddle reining Sandy around south, toward home. After nudging him into a trot he looked over his shoulder and returned the wave of the rancher and his wife.

"Let's go home Sandy. I'm sure there are more bad guys to chase down."

Chapter Seventeen

Dusk found an exhausted Tye about twenty or so miles from Fort Clark and his family. He had not had any rest so to speak in the last three days so he decided rather than push on he'd make camp and try and get a good night's sleep. Just as he was about to dismount and lead Sandy away from the road he saw two riders coming towards him. He watched for a few seconds. As he watched, something was familiar with the way the man in the lead sat his horse. A minute later Tye recognized the man as his former scout, Dan August. He didn't recognize the other man.

"What in the heck are you doing out here Dan?" Tye asked as he dismounted to meet the men.

Shaking hands Dan said. "Looking for you for this feller." He nodded toward the other man. "Tye this here is Sam Jenkins, Texas Ranger. Sam this is Tye Watkins." The two men shook hands.

"Why are you looking for me?"

Dan answered. "I'll let the ranger tell you."

Sam said. "About twenty years ago a small wagon train of settlers were ambushed by the Comanche up north of here just south of Palo Duro Canyon in the Texas Panhandle. All were killed but one boy of about seven. The boy's name was Jamie Kindle. His parents Bill and Allie Kindle along with a sister were among those killed. Jamie apparently showed a lot of adaptability over the years and became a warrior-quite a good one evidently. No one knows what happened for sure but he was apparently kicked out of his tribe for some reason and is now roaming the countryside alone and killing everyone he meets, both red and white; men ,women, children, hell he even kills the livestock for Christ's sake. His Comanche name is Two Bears., and the bastard has done killed two ranger friends of mine that were hunting him.

Tye nodded. "Sounds like a bad one, but what does that have to do with me?"

"Captain McNelly sent me to find you to see if you could track the bastard down and either kill him or bring him in to hang." He handed a telegram to Tye.

Tye Watkins
 Fort Clark, Tx

You are to assist the Texas Rangers in any way you can STOP Send report of progress as soon as you can END

William Alexander
Attorney General

Tye folded the telegram and stuffed it in his shirt pocket. "Where do we start?"

"Most of the killings have been west of Fort Stockton. We're to go there and report to the post commander for any late developments. We can stock up on supplies there to."

"I'm a little short on supplies and Fort Stockton is at least a hard two day ride from here," Tye said.

Sam patted his saddle bag. "I've coffee, biscuit, and jerky enough for the both of us for the trip."

Tye nodded. "It'll be dark in another twenty minutes so let's make camp and get an early start."

Sam nodded. "Sounds good."

They found a spot a couple hundred yards off the road and built a small fire and boiled some coffee. Sitting around the fire Tye wanted to know what was going on at the fort.

"Yahzie made an appearance on this side of the border," Dan said.

Tye almost choked on coffee he had just sipped. "Yahzie! What was he doing over here? He gave me his word he would not come back."

"Don't get your bowels in an uproar," Dan chuckled. "He heard the same news we did that Quanah Parker was leading a large band of Comanche down to take Apache kids and women."

"I heard that before I left," Tye interrupted.

"Well it was true and you ain't gonna believe what happened," Dan said shaking his head. "We, that's the U.S. Calvary, teamed up with Yahzie and his men and sent the Comanche and Parker lighting a shuck out of that part of Texas. He left damn near half his warriors dead."

The Calvary and the Apache fought side by side?" Tye questioned.

"Just about." Dan said. "The Apache ambushed Quanah and we cut off his escape or at least tried to. We killed about as many as the Apache did. It'll be a cold day in hell before the Comanche come back."

"I'll be damned," Tye said laughing. "Who was leading the column?"

" Captain McClellan."

Tye laughed even louder. "A year and a half ago he would never have dreamed he would be fighting alongside the Apache. Back then he went strictly by the manual and fighting side by side with your enemy I don't believe is in the manual." He laughed even harder. He got himself composed after a minute or so. "Did Major Thurston know about this?

"Only when we, Captain McClellan and me, gave him the report."

"And?"

"He did the same as you did. At first, disbelief and then laughed his ass off."

"What about you?" Sam asked. "Did you find Gillespie?"

"Tye related the story of his tracking Jack, the fight with the Apaches and his killing of the outlaw. "I was going to send the report in when I got to Clark." He looked at Dan. "Why don't you get Thurston to send the report in on Jack and the Frazier brothers when you get back and tell him to add to the report that I am with the rangers tracking down the Kindle kid that is called Two Bears."

"I'll see to it," Dan said.

It's late," Tye said looking up and judging the time by the stars. "Let's turn in and get an early start."

Sam lay there a long time with sleep eluding him. His thoughts were of Bill Herring and Lester Pickle the two rangers that son-of-a-bitch half-breed killed. They had ridden a lot of trails together and shared many a camp fire. He was not what one would say close friends with either, but that didn't matter; they were Texas Rangers and they had been gunned down and he was going to see that the killer paid for it. What bothered him was both men were veterans of many battles, been in just about any situation one could come up with and both as tough as they come. Apparently this damn half-breed was smarter and tougher.

His thoughts turned to Tye. *From what I have heard about him he can be meaner than a cornered Apache and has the smarts to outwit any man he's tracking. From what*

Dan told me he can track a lizard across rocks and live off the land as well as any Apache. With my gun handling ability along with him I like our chances. He drifted off to a restless sleep with those thoughts.

A low cloud cover with a promise of rain greeted the men as they broke camp. Dan headed back to Fort Clark with a promise to see Rebecca and tell her where Tye was headed as well as get major Thurston to send Tye's reports in. Tye and Sam would head north a ways until they were out of these low mountains and then head northwest toward Fort Stockton.

Mid morning found the two lawmen searching for some place to protect themselves and the horses. Approaching them from the west was a menacing looking black cloud that reached several thousand feet above the mesquite and sage covered landscape. The rain wasn't what bothered them it was the lightning they could see flashing in the cloud. In fairly flat country it was dangerous for a man on horseback in an electrical storm like the one approaching them.

"There's an arroyo over there," Tye hollered over the rising wind pointing to his right. Arriving they saw the arroyo which had been cut into the terrain over thousands of years by water from storms like the one they were fixing to endure.

"What about the water that will be coming down this thing," Sam asked?

"It won't be here for a while," Tye answered as he dismounted. "Being below ground level will protect us from the lightning till the storm passes. We'll just have to watch for the water and be ready to scramble out before it gets to deep."

They put their slickers on and squatted next to the bank of the arroyo holding the reins of their horses just as the first drops of rain begin to fall. It was a slow steady rain for about five minutes then the bottom fell out and the rain blown by the wind which was now blowing so hard that the drops of rain stung the men's faces like small hail stones. When a bolt of lightning struck nearby with a thunderous crash of thunder both men almost lost their grips on the reins of the startled horses. Both hands were now required to hold their horses as there was a steady rumble of rolling thunder interrupted every few seconds by tremendous explosions that seemed to shake the ground.

Sam nudged Tye and nodded to their right. A wall of water was rushing down the cut toward them, but it was only about a foot high, but both men knew what was coming behind it; probably water that would be five or six foot deep and rolling fast enough to keep a horse from getting his footing. They would be washed down the cut a ways before they could get out-if they could get out.

Tye leaned over and shouted into Sam's ear. "We'll wait a few more minutes. Maybe the worst of the storm will move on before the next wall of water. Keep an eye up the draw for it." Sam nodded his understanding. Tye knew they were fortunate to find this place and doubly so that the side of the draw they had entered on was not near as steep as the side they had their backs against. It was mostly rock instead of mud and should allow them to scramble out without much trouble.

Five minutes later the worst of the storm had passed and Tye stood up to take a look around. As he stood Sam hollered. "Here it comes!"

Both men were immediately scrambling up the side of the arroyo leading the frightened horses. After what seemed an eternitywhich in reality was only a few seconds they were out and on level ground just as a fair size dead tree went by carried by the rushing waters which was now four or five foot deep.

"Whew, that was damn close," Sam said.

"That's what makes living worthwhile," a smiling Tye chuckled. "Makes a man appreciate life all that more."

Sam looked at him with a 'wonder what the hell he's talking about' expression and then nodded his head when the meaning of what Tye said became plain to him. "Damned if it doesn't," he said laughing. "Damned if it doesn't." He liked this big-assed scout.

Chapter Eighteen

The rain slowed the trip to Fort Stockton by a day longer than the two had planned on. Several times they had to wait for a creek to recede enough for them to safely cross. They rode into the fort at mid-afternoon on the third day tired and ready for something to eat other than jerky and biscuits. First things first though so they headed to the post headquarters to speak with the Post Commander, Major Jeff Harwell, to get the latest news of the whereabouts of Jamie kindle or Two Bears or whatever the hell he was known by.

Major Harwell was a far cry from Major Thurston Tye thought as the major stood up from behind his desk as the two lawmen were ushered into his office by a skinny corporal. He was a couple inches short of six foot, but weighed about two hundred and forty or so pounds. He had a round face to go with his belly and the ruddy red tinged cheeks let it be known he probably liked his liquor. When Tye shook his hand it was like shaking a woman's hand, smooth and soft. Tye figured it had been weeks; maybe months since this man had been in the field or on a horse.

His desk was a mess with papers and a couple maps scattered so that very little of the desk top showed. He had an unlit cigar jutting out the corner of his mouth which he removed before he spoke.

"Sit down men. I've been expecting you for a couple days."

"Storm sorter slowed us down some Major," Tye said as he sat down on the straight back wooden chair next to Sam.

"It's a pleasure meeting you Mr. Watkins. I guess every officer in Texas has heard of your exploits along the border."

"Well, don't believe everything you hear major. Soldiers sometimes exaggerate things like the writers do in the dime novels," Tye chuckled.

"Come on Tye, don't be so modest, "Sam said smiling and then looked at the major. "Every story you have heard is probably true and more than likely has been toned down because no one would believe the actual truth. I got this straight from Major Thurston the Post Commander at Fort Clark. This man has done some remarkable things. Hell, he's only been a Deputy U.S. Marshall for two weeks and has already captured the Frazier gang and killed Bloody Jack Gillespie. I'd been proud do have done either one of those things."

"Well regardless of whether they are true or not there has been a lot of excitement on the fort since the news came you were coming. I don't expect you will get much rest with everyone wanting to talk to you," the major stated with a big smile still spread across his fat face.

"What's the latest on this Kindle fellow?" Sam asked.

Harwell shook his head. "Hadn't heard a word in a few days. Last report was of a homestead about fifteen miles due west that he had hit, or supposedly it was him. All the signs pointed to him as the culprit."

"What signs major," Tye asked?

"Everyone dead. The woman raped and her throat slashed. Two dead children and the most telling fact, all the livestock were killed. That's what he does. He's one crazy sonofabitch for sure."

Tye smiled. It was unusual for an officer to curse, but in the case of this killer, he thought the major's assessment was right on. "I guess you sent a patrol out."

Harwell looked at Tye and spat out, "Of course I did," his tone showing his anger at such a question. "They came back the next day with the same damn news they had at the other scenes of this crazy killer; nothing-no tracks, just dead bodies." He rested his elbows on the desk and buried his head in the palms of his hands. "I need something Tye-I need some good news, any news to tell the folks living around here who are scared to death. Hell, more families are coming here every day for protection. We're going to run out of room pretty quick. I hope you and Sam can help us out-help me out."

"That's what we were sent to do major. Can you see to it our horses are fed, watered, and bedded down till we leave and we need to go ahead and get some supplies so we can leave the moment news of his whereabouts comes in."

"You mean you aren't going to go looking for him now?"

Sam spoke up. "Major," he said sweeping his arms in a circular motion, "This here is a big country. Suppose we go west and he hits a family east of here. By the time you get the news to us and we backtrack to where the latest killings took place it might be three or four days; too late to track a man with a trail that cold. If we are here when the news arrives we can jump right on it and maybe pickup a fresh trail."

The major rubbed his beefy double chin. "I see what you mean. I'll see to it that your horses are taken care of and supplies are put in your bags for the pack horse. I'll have Corporal Sadler show you to your quarters where you can stay until you need to leave. At the rate he's killing it probably won't be a long wait"

The two lawmen stood up along with the major and shook hands. "I'll get word to you as soon as I hear anything." Both men nodded and left with the corporal.

Their quarters turned out to be a small room with one window and two beds that had straw filled mattresses that were lumpy as hell. There were pegs on the wall to hang hats, coats, gun belts, but no closet. There was one rickety table that had a bar of soap, a wash rag laying on top and one chair that had a towel hanging over the back. The corporal had offered his apologies but this was all they had at present.

"Not exactly a first class hotel room is it," Sam chuckled.

"Guess it's better than sleeping on the ground," Tye said feeling of the mattress, then added, "Maybe." He laughed.

Tye pulled his dirty, sweaty shirt off and walking outside to the pump he filled the wash basin. As usual when a man sees Tye without his shirt they are amazed at his build and scars. Sam was no different. He had never seen a man with a chest, shoulders, and arms like Tye and sure as hell had never saw a man with so many scars. Tye walked back in carrying the basin and noticed Sam looking at him.

"Every damn scar has a story Sam."

"Excuse me for looking Tye, but how in hell are you still alive?"

Tye laughed. "Old sawbones at Fort Clark says I ain't got any vital organs in me."

"Damn!" Sam exclaimed. "I sure believe it. Those from Apaches?"

"Mostly," Tye said. "Bullets, knives, arrows, and one tomahawk."

Sam shook his head. "I'd like to hear about them, but we'd be here a week if you just told me about half of them," he said chuckling.

"Haw, there's not much to tell about them Sam. If a man's been hunted by and hunted Apaches as long as I have he's gonna have some scars."

Sam laughed loudly and said, "That's the biggest bunch of horse shit I ever heard. Any other man would be dead and scalped from any one of them." He shook his head again as Tye finished washing, drying off, and pulling a clean shirt on.

Sam washed and changed shirts also and then both men walked out into the bright sunlight and searing heat that was approaching one hundred degrees. Sam had his ranger badge on, but Tye did not have his marshal's badge visible; it was in his shirt pocket as had been his custom so far in this early stage of his marshaling career.

They walked to the road leading into the fort and asked the guard about a place to get something to eat and drink. He pointed to town, or a few scattered shacks and a few businesses one of which was a saloon with decent food.

Walking to the saloon several soldiers could be seen-mostly black soldiers.

"What's up with all the negro soldiers here?" Sam asked.

"Buffalo soldiers," Tye answered. "The ninth and tenth Calvary is here which is mostly made up of blacks. They have earned the respect of settlers and Indians alike for their bravery in battle."

"I'll be damned," Sam said chuckling. "I never would have believed it if I wasn't seeing it with my own two eyes-black soldiers protecting white settlers." He laughed and shook his head. "Who would have thought it?"

About a half days ride southwest of the fort two families, the Greer's and the Simpsons, were headed for the protection of the fort. Jim Greer and his wife of thirty-five years, Amanda, were in the lead wagon. Their two teenage sons walked beside the wagon. The wagon was heavily loaded with family heirlooms and other items that Amanda did not want destroyed if their home was attacked and burned while they were gone. They, like everyone else in this part of Texas, had heard about the murdering breed called Two Bears.

Walt Simpson and his wife of twenty nine years Patsy were in the wagon following the Greer's. Will Simpson, their only child rode a horse beside his parents' wagon daydreaming about meeting a young girl when they reached Fort Stockton. Will was eighteen and ready to meet someone his own age. Outside of his parents and one or two young cowboys passing by their homestead he had not spoken with anyone his age in almost eight months, and certainly no girl. With a little luck they could be at the fort by the time it was full dark.

A hundred yards ahead a small bridge over a fifteen foot deep ravine that allowed travelers to continue without having to detour three miles to a place where the ravine could be traversed. Fifty yards to the right of the bridge and concealed by sage and cactus, Two Bears smiled, waiting for the travelers. He checked his Henry to make sure it was fully loaded and waited. He smiled at what was going to happen to these unsuspecting white eyes. With his hatchet he had hacked two of the support post on the bridge just enough not to break until weight was applied to the planks on top. The weight of a wagon would do nicely. Two minutes more he figured. He had to stifle a laugh at how hapless these white eyes were fixing to be-and how dead.

Chapter Nineteen

Two Bears plan did not go exactly as planned. As soon as the weight of the horses was on the planks of the bridge the structure collapsed. The wagon tongue snapped as the horses plunged into the ravine. Jim was almost jerked from the seat when the reins he was holding suddenly jerked taut.

"What the hel…" he started to holler but never finished as a heavy .44 calibre slug from Two Bears rifle hit him in the right side of the head just above his ear and exited on the left side with a hole the size of a man's fist. Blood and gore sprayed on the two young boys who watched in horror as their father fell at their feet. Amada screamed as did Patsy in the second wagon.

Gary McMillan

Walt Simpson reined in his team. "Get down!" he screamed. "Get down and under the wagon!" Patsy was hysterical and Walt grabbed her to force her down just as a bullet struck her in the throat. "NO! NO!" Walt shouted as his wife collapsed in his arms. She looked up at him and tried to say something but only blood came out of her mouth. He hugged her to his chest and jumped to the ground just as another bullet slammed into the back of the wooden seat where he had been an instant before.

Walt laid his wife gently on the ground and for a moment he was paralayzed as to what had just happened then anger and hate took over and he snatched his rifle from the seat and turned toward where the shots had come from. He was trying to locate the exact spot when a puff of smoke appeared followed by the crack of a Henry. Out of the corner of his eye he saw one of Jim's boys go down. He fired five or six shots where he saw the smoke as fast as he could pull the lever oh his new Henry.

Two Bears had dropped into the ravine as soon as he had fired and this action saved him as the bullets from the white man's gun ripped the area where he had been. He ran past the struggling horses in the ravine that were screaming in pain from broken legs. He found a spot where he could climb up the wall and reaching the top smiled again. Forty feet in front of him was the wife of the first man he had shot huddled with her remaining son. The other lay by her husband. He studied her and saw she was fairly old. He aimed his Henry and squeezed the trigger. The rifle butt slammed into his shoulder and the 44 slug found it mark just under the woman's hairline. He worked the lever and squeezed off another shot and the boy lay beside his mother. Two Bears ducked just as a bullet cut the air by his ear. He slipped back down into the ravine and moved back to where he had been before and climbing back up was once again hidden in the sage and cactus.

He smiled. "This white man has warrior blood in him," he mumbled to himself." I will enjoy killing him but it will not be a quick death."

Thirty minutes passed-then forty-five. "I think he has gone pa." Will said standing up.

"No Will! Get dow…" A bullet struck Will in the chest knocking him off his feet. Walt scrambled over to him and placing his hand under the boys head raised him up. Will grabbed Walt's shoulder. "Pa…P…" and he died.

Walt looked at the body of his wife and then at his son. He looked up to see Jim and Amanda lying dead with their son. "You sorry son of a bitch" he screamed and charged the ravine where he last saw the smoke from the rifle. The problem was Two Bears had moved again. He had his sights on the white man's chest, but lowered them and shot him in the knee. Walt screamed and dropping his rifle grabbed his knee as he crumbled to the hard ground. A second later he realized his mistake and started looking for the gun. As he twisted his body to look behind him he saw the grinning face of Two Bears and then nothing. Two Bears had slammed the butt of the Henry into Walt's head knocking him out. The breed drug the limp body to the wagon and finding some rope tied the white man to one of the wheels. He walked to the ravine and shot the injured horses. He then walked back to the wagon Walt was tied too and shot those horses. He scalped each of the dead bodies and laid them on the ground in from of the unconscious white man.

He walked to the water barrel and taking the metal dipper that hung on the side filled it and drank deeply. He then walked around to the white man and threw water in his face to wake him up. Walt opened his eyes slowly and shook his head trying to clear his brain. He wished he hadn't. The first thing he saw was the scalps of his wife, son and friends. He looked up into the grinning face of Two Bears and knew he was in for it. The bastard had a knife and squatted down in front of Walt. Using the tip of the razor sharp blade he cut the buttons off Walt's shirt and jerked it open.

"I'm not going to give you the pleasure of screaming like a woman you bastard," he shouted and spit in the breeds face. Two Bears grinned again as he wiped the spittle off his face.

"White man brave. We see how brave." He stuck the blade deep into Walt's shoulder and twisted it. Walt's eyes bulged and sweat broke out on his forehead, but he didn't make a sound. Two Bears sat back on his haunches smiling. "Now we see," He said. He reached down and undid the belt buckle andhad just began pulling Walts's pants down when he heard horses.

Lieutenant Fletcher was leading a patrol were taking a break when they heard the rifle fire.

"Too many shots to be a hunter Lieutenant," Sergeant Cranston noted.

"Get the men mounted Sergeant." A few seconds later they were galloping down the road in the direction the shots came from. Sergeant Cranston, riding beside the lieutenant shouted over the thundering of hooves.

"Sounds like they came from about where the bridge is sir." Fletcher nodded and kicked his mount into more speed. If this was Two Bears he was closer to him than any other officer had been and by damn he wasn't going to let him get away. He would probably get a field promotion for killing the murdering savage.

Fletcher had graduated from the Point fifth in his class two years earlier. So far, his tenure on the frontier had been less than exciting. He had been on countless patrols and so far had not seen a single hostile. The only time his Navy Colt had been fired was on the firing range. He was more than anxious to prove himself to his superiors and to the men he led-too anxious has it worked out.

Two Bears cursed under his breath as he saw the blue clad soldiers coming fast down the road. He quickly mounted his pony and looking at the man tied to the wagon wheel. He lifted the Henry and shot him in the other shoulder just to make him suffer. He kicked his pony into a hard run and disappeared in the sage, cedars, and mesquite. Twenty seconds later Fletcher and the patrol arrived and surveyed the carnage and then
Fletcher seeing Walt jumped from his mount and rushed to him.

"Good God!" he shouted. "He's alive." Sergeant Cranston was quickly by the lieutenants side. They cut the ropes and lay Walt flat on the ground and Cranston picked up the man's hat and stuck it under his head for a pillow.

"Who did this man?" Fletchers asked.

"Th…Think it was an Injun," the barely conscious man whispered struggling to fight off the pain.

"What do you mean you think it was an Indian?"

The man was struggling to talk through the pain. " He…he looked like he had…" his voice cracked as a new wave of pain hit him. " Looked like he was part white."

Fletcher looked in the direction they had seen the rider leave. "Two Bears."

Fletcher knew Cranston was pretty good at doctoring. Sergeant, get a man to stay here with you and take care of this man's wounds the best you can and then get him to the fort. The rest of us are going to run that bastard down."

"Yes, sir. You be careful sir. He's one mean son-of-a-bitch." Fletcher nodded and jumped in the saddle and he and three men left in pursuit of the breed called Two Bears.

Cranston got the bleeding stopped in Walt's shoulders but the bullet did not go through and was still in the shoulder wound.

"I know you are in a lot of pain sir," Cranston said, "But we have got to get you to the fort and the hospital.

This is going to hurt but we've got to lift you into the back of the wagon." Private Linder had spread several blankets in the bed of the wagon after throwing stuff out to make room. Walt screamed when they lifted him and mercifully passed out. They placed their mounts in the wagons harnesses in place of the ones that had been shot. Cranston knew where they had to go to cross the ravine and cursed the breed again because of the delay it would cause in getting this man to the fort.

Two Bears reined his mount to a halt and jumping down quickly, he ran back to the top of the hill he had just ridden over. Kneeling behind a thick cedar he watched his back trail. In less than a minute he saw the four riders coming fast following his trail. The warrior smiled when he saw them.

"No scout, just foolish bluecoats," he muttered out loud and then laughed. *No scout will make them easy for Two bears to trap and kill,* he thought to himself as he ran back down the slope to his pony. Jumping easily on the pony's back he headed away from the oncoming soldiers, but he made sure he left a trail that even a bluecoat could follow.

A half mile from the hill he found what he was looking for; a arroyo deep enough for him to be concealed with brush growing along the rim. It was deep enough to hide his pony also. He quickly found a way into it and dismounting found a good place to shoot from. He waited. He knew it would not be long because he could hear the hoof beats of the stupid soldier's horses. He checked his Henry and found out he hadn't reloaded. He quickly shoved some .44 caliber shells in and worked the lever to put a shell in the chamber. He was ready.

Lieutenant Fletcher led his men at a fast canter now and he was spending most of his time looking at the ground following the tracks. Private Langley, a veteran of many a patrol and skirmishes with the Apache and the Comanche knew they were headed for trouble going headlong like they were. He pulled his Sharps carbine from its leather and rode with the butt on his right thigh the barrel pointed toward the sky and cocked, and his finger on the trigger. The other two men noticing the veteran did the same.

They had no more than rested the butts of their Sharps on their thighs than all hell broke loose. The lieutenant flipped backwards off his horse like a giant hand had swatted him. The crack of the rifle followed instantly and then more firing. Langley was swept out of his saddle his head exploding like a melon dropped on a rock. The other two swapped directions and lit a shuck out of the trap.

Two Bears took a deep breath and let it out slow as he aimed the Henry. It bucked against his shoulder and the heavy slug burned through the air and hit one of the soldiers in the middle of the back. He threw his arms up fell forward on his horse's neck. He held on to the pommel of his saddle to keep himself from falling off. The other man, Private Anderson, seeing his buddy hit, reached over and holding him by the collar helped him stay in the saddle. Anderson flinched when another slug burned his right shoulder and then they were over a hill and out of range. He slowed the tired mounts to a trot and then a walk glancing every few seconds over his shoulder praying he did not see that crazy breed chasing them. His shoulder burned like the blazes and his friend was in bad shape. He knew he was several hours from the fort and he did not plan on stopping till he got there.

"The Great Spirit is smiling on me this day," Two Bears said when he saw the leader of the blue coats was not dead. His bullet had creased his skull and he was just unconscious. Two Bears retrieved the lieutenant's horse and lifted the unconscious man up and laid him across the saddle, belly down. He took some rawhide and tied his hands and then running the rawhide under the horses belly he tied the other end to the man boots and pulled it tight, securing the man to the saddle. Mounting his pony he headed into the hills, away from the road.

~~

It was dusk when a private came to Tye's and Sam's quarters and knocked on the door which was partially open.

"Mr. Watkins Sur. The major says come quick."

"Did he say why?"

"No Sur. He just told me to get you two to him quick like."

The two lawmen followed the young black private to post headquarters.

"What is it major?" Tye asked as soon as they were ushered into Harwell's office.

"Two Bears just killed several civilians west of here. A patrol led by a very young Lieutenant Fletcher happened to be close by and arrived in time to see the killer fleeing. They found two families murdered. One man survived, a Walt Simpson. He lost his wife and son to the murdering breed. He was tied to a wagon wheel and was fixing to be tortured when Fletcher and his men came on the scene. Lieutenant Fletcher dispatched Sergeant

Cranston and another man to doctor Simpson up best they could and get him back here. He took out after the breed with the three remaining men."

"This Lieutenant Fletcher an experienced officer?" Tye questioned.

Major Harwell leaned forward and put the palms of his hands on the desk and lowered his eyes to the desktop.

"No. He has been out here awhile, but he has had no experience with Indians or bandits. I sent him with Sergeant Cranston who is one of my best men to keep him out of trouble and what does he do-he orders Cranston back here."

"I've got a feeling major that young Fletcher bit off more than he can chew." The major nodded his agreement.

"Sergeant Cranston wants to lead you to where all this took place. I've told him to take three good men with him and find Fletcher and the others and assist you in any way they can to bring that murdering breed in. They will be under your orders."

"When can they be ready to leave?" Tye asked.

"They should be outside now with yours and Sam's horses along with a pack mule and supplies for a week."

Sam started for the door. "What the hell are we waiting for? Let's get after him."

Tye nodded to the major and followed Sam out the door. They stopped by their quarters on the way out of the fort and picked up their saddle bags and Henry's.

~~

Dusk found Two Bears sitting by a small fire pondering what to do with the soldier lying on his stomach a few feet from him. Fletcher had regained consciousness a little earlier but quickly decided he was better off if the breed didn't know it so he pretended to be out. He watched the man by barely opening one eye, peering through the narrow slit. He also knew he was going to be tortured and silently cursed his stupidity and arrogance and then wished like hell he was already dead. He had heard stories of the terrible things the Redman could do to prisoners and there was not one thing he could do to prevent it. He wondered about the men that were with him. He figured they were dead or they would have showed themselves by now. A sudden thought occurred to him that gave him hope. What if they were out there now, watching, waiting for a chance to help him. Maybe they…he didn't finish that thought as he saw the breed get up and walk his way.

God help me, he prayed silently. His eyes flew open as all the wind went out of him when the breed kicked him hard in the stomach. He tried to get his breath, sucking in great amounts of air. A minute later he had regained his composure and opened his eyes again and was the breed squatting in front of him sharpening his knife. "Oh God" he cried.

Two Bears chuckled. "White man's God not going to help you now."

Chapter Twenty

Camp had been made shortly before full dark and now Tye, Sam and the soldiers sat around a small fire whose flames were mostly hidden from preying eyes by rocks stacked around it. The men held steaming cups of coffee and sipped slowly to keep from scalding their tongues and throats. There wasn't much talk around the fire as the three buffalo soldiers were lamenting over their friend who they had buried a few yards away and concerned about the lieutenant whose body they did not find.

"Whatcha think our chances are of catching up with that son-of-a-bitch." Sergeant Cranston asked looking directly at Tye.

Tye waited a moment taking another sip of coffee before answering. "If he can't fly, we'll track him down," he answered. He took another sip and pitched the remaining amount on the ground. "I don't know if it will be in time to help the lieutenant though,"

One of the soldiers looked up. "Yu rekon tha he's still alive Mr. Watkins sur?"

Tye stood up and walked toward the soldiers and squatted down in front of them. "You men liked the lieutenant?"

"Yes sur, we surely do. He one of the few officers who showed us respect. Yes Sur, we all like him."

"You might just add him to your prayer list tonight then. If he's alive, he's going to a have a rough time of it. I hope you don't think bad of me for saying this, but if a man has a choice of being dead or a captive of the Indians, he's better off being dead."

There was a long moment of silence before anyone spoke. One of the soldiers poked the fire with a stick. "We knows what you mean Mr. Watkins. We wus thankin tha same thang."

"Being at Fort Clark for the last few years I have had the privilege of being around some mighty find soldiers-men to ride the river with," Tye said. "I can tell you men are cut from the same mold. I'm goanna do my dammdest to find that breed and your lieutenant and just hope we are in time to save him."

Tye walked off to where the horses were picketed to check on Sandy. Cranston looked at Sam and in a low voice asked.

"All the stories about that man true?"

Sam filled his cup with the last of the coffee. "Hadn't known him for long, but I talked to the Post Commander, Major Thurston, and Dan August his number one scout in length about him. I'd say most of them are and like Dan told me, the stories have been toned down some because no one would believe them otherwise. We changed clothes and washed up when we first arrived at Stockton and I was plumb embarrassed. He has muscles where you and I could only dream about having. And scars, my God, he has more gunshot wounds, knife wounds, and arrow wounds than the whole damn bunch of soldiers at Clark put together." He chuckled and added. "I asked him how in hell he was still alive and he said that the post surgeon told him he would never die because he had no vital organs."

All the men laughed just as Tye was walking back into the firelight. "Did I miss something?"

Cranston, still laughing, straightened up and said. "Sam just told us what the doc said about you having no vital organs."

"I don't," Tye said with a straight face. "No heart, no lungs, but I do have a lot of bullshit in me." The remark cracked everyone up. Tye laughed with the rest then said. "We're going to get an early start so let's turn in. Sergeant, set up a schedule for sentry. I'll take the last watch." Tye always took the last one when he could. It had been his experience that if anything was going to happen it was usually a little before first light when camps were sleeping the soundest.

Tye placed a few small dead sticks on last night's still smoldering coals. He stirred the coals with another stick and soon had a small fire. He placed the coffee pot on the rocks after filling it with water. When the water was boiling he dropped in a good handful of coffee grounds and then after waiting a moment he set the coffee pot away from the fire and dropped in cold water to settle the grounds. He poured himself a cup and as he raised it to his lips his eyes fell on four men sitting up in their bedrolls. He chuckled to himself. *Smell of coffee wakes up a soundly sleeping man quicker than anything other than an Apache charge.*

"You boys going to sleep the day away?" he questioned, smiling as he said it.

"No Sur, we ain't Mr. Tye. We's jus't wait'n fer you ta make us sum of that there coffee," the black soldier named Wes said. Tye didn't remember his last name but he appeared to be the oldest. After everyone poured himself a cup nothing was said as they sipped. Tye studied the men over the brim of his cup. *Cranston looks like a man that will be a soldier till he dies,* he thought. *I'd be willing to bet he's a top soldier and probably has been busted a few times like most good sergeants he has known. He looked the type that had no backing down in him once he made up his mind about something.* He took a sip and studied the three black soldiers. He had heard about them, but this is the first time he had been around any. He was impressed by these three and figured the stories about how well these men known as buffalo soldiers fought were true. The Indians he heard respected them as fighting men which is more than can be said for a lot of white troops. For the most part, the Redman had nothing but disdain for the fighting ability of the regular army. *I can understand their thinking about the white soldiers to a point. I've seen some run and*

*cower shaking like a leaf in the wind when Apaches strike.
I've heard them screaming like a woman when tortured,
something you would never see an Apache do. The Apache
has seen men shoot themselves when it looks like they were
going to be captured. This, to them was the sign of a
coward and usually they would not even touch the body
other than to spit on the corpse.*

Sam broke the silence. "Looks like you're in some
deep thought Tye."

Tye emptied his cup on the ground. "No," he lied,
"Just thinking we need to get moving following the breed,"
he said standing up and walking to the horses. He saddled
Sandy, stepped into the saddle. He watched as the men
shook out their boots to make sure no unfriendly critters
had found a home for the night in them before pulling them
on. They moved out just as the gray streaks of dawn
appeared over the hills.

About noon Tye raised his hand and the little group
halted. Tye sat for a moment. To the others it appeared he
was sniffing the air.

"What is it Tye?" Sam asked.

"Thought I got a whiff of a campfire. Ya'll rest
here while I take a look see. He nudged Sandy and moved

forward with his Henry in his hand after levering in a .44 cal. cartridge.

"I don't smell nut'in," the soldier named James said after Tye rode away.

"Me neither,"Cranston said," but we're going to wait and see." He pulled his Sharps from the leather and checked it. The others seeing this did the same. Sam already had his Henry out.

Five anxious minutes later Tye appeared on the crest of a low hill about a hundred yards away. He stood in his stirrups and motioned with his Henry to come on.

When they arrived where Tye sat on Sandy they gathered around him. "The breeds camp was at the bottom of this hill." He looked at each of the soldiers for a moment without saying anything.

"It's tha lieutenant ain't it Mr. Watkins," Wes said fearing the worst.

Tye nodded. "I'm going to tell you men to prepare yourself because it's not pretty. The lieutenant had a rough night, but let me tell you something else. Over the years I've grown to know the Apaches and Comanche pretty well and I can tell you this, your Lieutenant Fletcher died well. An Indian believes a man who he is torturing strength will flow into his own body and make him stronger. The longer he tortures the more this strength will flow. If the man cowers and whimpers like a woman he will just kill him right off because the man had no strength. Your Lieutenant Fletcher was not a man who had no strength. He died well." Tye could see the disappointment in the soldier's faces, then Wes spoke.

"Knew he would Sur. We's wus just hoping by sum miracle we wud find him alive." They rode down the slope into the camp.

"Oh my God!" one of the soldiers cried out. "Look what that bastard dun did to our lieutenant." He stepped from his horse and lost what little was on his stomach. Sam and the other two just sat there staring at what was once a man saying nothing.

Fletcher, or what was a man named Fletcher, was tied to a mesquite and stripped naked. Both ears had been cut off and a lot of skin on his chest had been peeled away. One eye had been dug out with a knife and a fire had been set between his legs. Tye had never seen a man tortured this bad and he had seen a lot. *This breed has a lot of hate in him; more than I have ever seen,* he thought. *There has to be a reason for this,* he thought to himself.

As the others sat on their horses and the one on his knees sat in stunned silence Tye dismounted and stood in front of the men between them and where the lieutenant was. "There has to be a reason for this much hate in a man. Sam, and I'm asking you. What caused this man to start killing people and why like this? He asked pointing to Fletcher. I've seen a hundred men that had been tortured but not to this extent. Why?"

"The only thing I know is that someone raped his wife and thirteen year old daughter before killing them."

"Vengeance," Tye spit out the word. "He's killing out of vengeance and doesn't care if he's caught or killed because he feels he has nothing to live for. Damn! That makes him even more dangerous."

He walked to Sandy. Ya'll bury the lieutenant while I try and pick up this bastards trail. He mounted and started circling the camp.

Wes sighed as he looked at Fletcher. "Let's bury the lieutenant boys and then we'll say a few words over him." They set about the task with no words being spoken among them. Sam noticed how gently they handled the body.

Those boys really cared for the officer, he thought to himself. The soldier's scratched out a shallow hole with sticks and lay Fletcher in it gently after wrapping him in a blanket. They covered the body with dirt and then lay rocks on top to keep the varmints away.

"Lord," Wes said as the men stood around the makeshift grave with their hats in their hands and heads bowed, "Tha lootenant wus a good man, Lord. He treated ev'er man tha same which'in more than yu can sau for most white folk. He shor didn't deserv ta die like this. His sufferin's over now Lord so take our friend to Yur bosom and make him whole aga'n. Protek an keep him safe. Amen." His amen was followed by a chorus of others just as they heard a horse coming up. Tye dismounted and walked to where the men were and took off his hat. As they stood there Tye spoke in a low, reverent tone looking down at the grave.

"I didn't know this man Lord, but I know what kind of a man he was because of what these good men he led said about him. I don't pretend to know his relationship with You but I'm asking You Lord, as a favor Lord, take him and keep him. I know You need good men up there just like we do down here." He then led the men in the Lord's Prayer.

He turned and walked off putting his hat on his head.

Wes turned to Sam. "I don't kno yet kno whut kind of fight'n man he is, but he's one fine man to kno. That wus nice whut he said abut tha lootenant and sumthang he shor didn't hav'ta do. Shor nice ta find a man like him out here."

"What do mean by that?"

"A man we hear can fight like an Indian, track bett'n most uf them, meener than a she bear with cubs, and kno's tha scripture."

"You will learn what every man, woman, child, and soldier along the border knows; he's a special man and as good a man as he is, he's a man you don't want to tangle with in any kind of fight. He can track a lizard over rocks, as good as or better than any Apache with a knife, he's a crack shot with a pistol and rifle, never lost a stand up knock'um down fist fight and never shot a man in the back."

Wes looked at Sam. "Thought yu only knowed him a few days?"

"Have," Sam said smiling. "Long enough to know everything I and you have heard about him is gospel true." He looked at the other men. "Any of you could have followed the breed's track and found this camp because I sure couldn't. Most of the time I could not see anything of a trail or track till he pointed it out."

"We were wundering if he wus following him most of tha time to," Lester said. "He made believers out of us when he found this here camp. He shor'nuf can track and that's a fact."

"Lets get mounted and follow our scout," Sam said, putting his hat on and walking to where their horses were picketed. "I want that son-of-a-bitch dead more than ever now."

Chapter Twenty One

The homestead was not much to look at from where Two Bears sat. He sat on a knoll about a hundred yards east of the home hidden by some thick sage brush and a couple cedars. He sat cross-legged with his Henry across his lap. He had been watching the place for a couple hours. He didn't figure they had much but he had spotted a fine looking sorrel in the corral, but the horse took second fiddle to a young girl with red hair he was watching hanging some clothes up to dry in the heat of the sun. He couldn't tell how old she was, not that it mattered, but she looked to have all the curves in the right spots. There appeared to be a man of the house, his wife, the girl, and a boy of about ten or so living there. He decided he would watch a little longer to make sure no one else was about and make his move after dark. He watched the girl and licked his lips in anticipation.

Tye was leading the men at a good clip as the breed was making no effort to cover his tracks. *This man is either the most careless man I have ever known or the dumbest,* he thought. *Or maybe he just doesn't think anyone would be on his trail this quick. Then there is the possibility he knows we are following him and just waiting for the right time to pick us off.* That thought sent a chill up his spine and he reined Sandy in and stepped down, dropping the reins as he kneeled down to study the tracks closer. Sam and the others reined in and sat watching for a moment. Sam took a plug of tobacco out of his shirt pocket and bit off a chew and offered some to the soldiers who all shook their heads.

He chewed for a moment; spit a brown stream at a rock and spoke.

"You want to clue us in on what you are thinking there, Marshall?"

Tye continued to study the tracks for a moment then answered. "We're only about three hours behind him. He's in no hurry and not bothering to attempt to hide his trail."

He stood up and turned to face the men. "If you had just killed a family plus no telling how many more would you just ride as if you were on a Sunday stroll and not seem to care if anyone was following or not?"

Les spoke up. "Wal sir. If'in it was me I'd be lit'ng a shuck fer places unknown and be in wun hell uf a hurry ta git thar."

"So would I," Tye said. "And that bothers me. He's either crazy, don't give a damn, or just don't think anyone would be chasing him. Then there's the other thing." Tye added.

"What's that?" Sam asked shifting the chaw from one side of his mouth to the other.

"He knows he's being followed and is waiting for the right time and place to set a trap." The soldiers and Sam all quickly looked around nervously.

"You think one man would take on the five of us?" Sam asked spitting another stream of tobacco.

"This hombre doesn't give a damn Sam. He doesn't care if he lives or dies and that's what makes him so dangerous. Everything has been taken from him that he cared about so he's just killing and will keep killing till he's killed. I guarantee he won't give up no matter what the circumstances are. We'll have to kill him."

"Counted on that," Sam said.

Tye mounted Sandy and headed west. "Let's go, but you boys don't doze back there. I suggest you keep an eye out for trouble because we are damn sure headed for it."

Thirty minutes before the sun would drop behind the hills, Tye reined in and stepped down from Sandy. Sam and the others sat on their horses a few feet away. They had remembered Tye's scolding them for gathering around him when he was reading sign. After q moment Tye stood up and looked west toward the setting sun. The men dismounted and walked their mounts to where he and Sandy stood.

"We'll leave the horses in that stand of cedar over there," he said pointing to the left of where they were. The men saw a thick stand of cedars many of which were seven or eight feet tall with some bunch grass around them. "Tie your horses with enough rope that lets them move around some but don't tie them so well they can't get loose."

"Why the hell do that," Sam asked spitting the ever present stream of tobacco juice.

"If you don't come back you don't want your horse to starve to death do you?"

"What the hell are you talking about? Come back from where?"

"See that pile of horse manure over there," Tye said pointing to it. "If you look at it real close I'd say it was less than an hour old." The men straightened up and things got quiet. "I think we will go a ways on foot. We can move a lot quieter that way." He looked at Cranston. "Pick a man to stay here with the horses. I wouldn't want that breed to double back and run them off. The rest of you follow me and be damn quiet. If I stop, you stop. If I squat, you squat. Understood?" Each of the men nodded their understanding. "Bring your Sharps." Lester stayed with the horse's after Tye told him to hide himself in those rocks about twenty five yards away and stay alert. "You doze off just might not wake up," he added. Sam, Wes, James, and Cranston followed Tye.

A lot of animals have a sense of danger approaching. Most of your great fighting men, both Red and white, have it also, but to varying degrees. Men like Tye, Jim Bridger, and Kit Carson survived many Indian fights because of their fighting ability but they also kept themselves and others with them out of a lot of trouble by '*sniffing*' out pending trouble and avoiding it. Two Bears was one of those men.

As he watched the homestead below him a sudden feeling overcame him of pending danger. He turned his head slowly and looked over his right shoulder and saw nothing. Twisting his head and looking over his left shoulder he thought he saw movement through a stand of cedars. His horse was behind him to his right so he knew it was not his horse. *A deer maybe,* he pondered. He shifted his body very slowly to where he could shoot if necessary. He knew quick movement could be spotted a lot easier than a slow, deliberate move.

Watching closely the first thing he saw was blue. *Soldiers!* They were about seventy yards away as he slowly raised the barrel of his Henry to his shoulder. He laid his cheek against the stock, put the front sight in the vee of the rear one, levered in a round, and waited. The only movement was his eyes. He ignored the pesky flies and gnats that buzzed around his face and hands. He loved this thing called ambush-he smiled.

Tye was to the end of the cedars that had been too thick to move quietly through. His next step would put him around them-suddenly he froze, the men behind him did likewise. A feeling of imminent danger had just hit him like a thunderbolt. He kelt down on one knee. The others did the same.

Cranston was the closest to Tye. "What is it Tye?" he whispered. "What's wrong?"

Tye looked at the men and put a finger to his lips indicating them to be quiet. He turned his head back to look where he had been going. He studied the brush on the hill across the way carefully.

Two Bears could not figure out why the soldiers had not appeared at the end of the cedars. He knew they had to be behind them. *Maybe they saw me and are trying to figure out what to do. He had them trapped.* A sloping hill was behind the men so if they tried to go that way he would have a clear shot at them over the tops of the cedars. He also would have a clear shot if they tried to go back where they had come from or if they went forward toward him. *What the hell,* the breed thought. *It's a good day to die.* He would fire several quick shots through the cedars. Maybe he would get lucky. He picked a spot about four feet above the ground and squeezed the trigger.

Tye was studying the brush and in particular a shadow behind some sage and in the shade of a very tall cedar. *God! That's a man with a rifle,* he thought as he figured out what the shadow was.

"On your bellies," he shouted an instant before the crack of the rifle.

Tow Bears followed his first shot with six more as fast as he could lever in another shell spacing the shots about three or four feet apart. He was elated when he heard a curse.

"Dammitt," Cranston uttered loudly as the forty-four slug hit him in the shoulder, just below his collar bone. The force of the bullet spun him around and onto his back.

"Lie still Cranston," Tye shouted. He turned back to where he was looking before and saw the haze of blue smoke from the rifle drifting away in the slight breeze. He could see the man was still there. He shifted his body a little and brought his Henry up and lined the man up in his sights. He was squeezing the trigger when a bullet kicked up dirt in his face and eyes blinding him. He cursed and rolled over on his back.

"You hit," Sam hollered.

"No," Tye answered. "Just a damn face full of dirt. He wiped his face with his kerchief and blinked a few times. Between his eyes watering and the kerchief he managed to get the dirt out of his eyes. He blinked a few times to help clear his vision and looked at the men huddled close to him.

"You men stay where you are except for you Wes. You crawl over to Cranston and see how bad he's hit. The rest of you wait here."

"What the hell are you going to do?" Sam asked.

"Look around Sam. The breed has us pinned down. I'm going to earn my pay and root him out." He bunched his legs under him preparing to spring out and charge the man.

"You can't do that he'll kill you for su..."Sam's word were lost in a hail of gunfire as Tye raised his Henry and fired, levered another round and fired and then took off firing more bullets as he ran. He saw the shadow twist and then turn and run to his right. Tye fired three more times at him through the sage brush and cedars, but knew he didn't hit him. He started after him, but stopped when he heard a horse running away.

"Damn...Dammitt to hell, Tye cursed knowing the man got away and they were twenty or so minutes from their horses. Sam and the others came running.

When they got to where Tye was they all saw the homestead and a man, woman and two young people watching. The man had what looked like a shotgun.

Tye spoke up and pointed to the ground. "The breed was going to kill that family down there. See the cigarette butts and here's the imprint of his butt as he sat and watched. I figure he was going to wait till dark and kill them. From the way it looks, he was here for a couple hours. We just busted up his party." Tye looked back to where Cranston lay. "You men go get our horses and put Cranston on one if he can ride and take him to the house down there. Sam and me will go down there and meet the family. He stood up and then stopped. "Looks like I winged him," he said pointing to a couple drops of blood on a rock. "Lets get on down there. Maybe the woman is good at nursing." He and Sam walked down the slope toward the homestead and the others went to get the horses and Cranston.

"That's far enough," the homesteader said when they were about twenty yards away. "Who are you and what you want."

Sam spit out his wad of tobacco. "Look at that girl," he said in a low voice. "Have you ever seen a prettier one." Tye didn't answer him.

"I'm Tye Watkins," he said loud enough for the family to hear. "Sam here," he said nodding to Sam and me are Deputy U.S. Marshalls.

"Heard of a Tye Watkins at Fort Clark," The man answered still holding the scattergun on the two men.

"I was a scout there till a few weeks ago before I took a marshaling job." About that time the blue clad soldiers came over the hill with the horses. Wes walked beside the horse Cranston was on helping him stay in the saddle.

The man held the scatter gun steady as he watched them and the soldiers. "We're chasing a breed called Two Bears, Tye said. "He was on the hill watching you and your family when we surprised him."

"What do you suppose he was doing up there?" the man asked and lowered the gun a little.

"He's murdered several families already. I figure he was waiting till dark and then going to do the same to you and yours."

"We don't have any money or anything like that."

"You have a fine looking horse and then he looked at the man's daughter, and a fine looking daughter."

The woman gasped and pulled her daughter to her as well as the young boy.

"You mean he would kill all of us for a horse and…" his voice trailed off as he looked at his daughter then back at Tye.

"I don't know how many exactly this breed has killed, but it's more than a few and he has killed for less."

"Is he crazy or what?" the man said lowering the barrel of the shotgun toward the ground. Sam breathed for the first time in what seemed like an eternity which is where he would have been if the man had accidently twitched his trigger finger.

"No he's not crazy; he's a man bent on vengeance for what some men did to his family and he's going to kill and keep killing till he's killed or captured."

"That poor soldier looks like he has been wounded," the woman said.

"Yes'um," Tye replied. "He was hit in all that gunfire you heard a few minutes ago."

"Well, get him down and in the house. After what ya'll did the least I can do is doctor him the best I can."

Wes and James help the groaning Cranston down and carried him to the house. The woman told them to put him in the chair by the window which they did.

"Sho' appreciate this ma'am," Wes said tipping his hat.

"You're more than welcome," the lady said as she cut Cranston's shirt away so she could look at the wound. She looked at the small purple hole in the front and the larger one in the back. "Looks like it went clean thru which is a good thing," she said. She held a small hand mirror and using the sun light coming through the window she directed the beam of light to the wound and bent close to inspect it. "You are a lucky man," she said smiling at Cranston. "I don't think it hit any bones directly. It might have barely touched your collar bone, but outside of the pain for awhile you should be fine."

"Thank you ma'am," Cranston said grimacing in pain. "Don't suppose you got any valium or something else for the pain do you?"

She shook her head. "All we have is a little rot gut whiskey my husband keeps around.

Cranston's eyes lit up. "Well I'm not a drinking man, but I think that would do just fine ma'am," he said licking his lips. Wes and James had to turn their heads so the lady would not see them laughing. Cranston had been in the guardhouse a dozen times for drinking and getting in fights.

"I'm Bill Schaffer and this here boy is Bill Jr. and this is my daughter Jenny. Sam ignored the man and boy and stuck out his hand to Jenny. Sam," he said. "My name is Sam," he repeated as he took the hand she offered him. Her touch sent a jolt up Sam's arm and into his heart. He had never seen a more beautiful woman in his life.

"Pleased to meet you Sam," she said holding on to this handsome stranger's hand a little longer than necessary.

"That's Elizabeth in there taking care of your man."

"Pleased to make your acquaintance Mr. Schaffer."

"Just call me Bill."

"Bill it is then," Tye said.

Tye walked over to Sandy and stepped into the saddle. Sam finally tore his eyes away from Jenny and looked at him.

"Where you going?"

"After the breed. You follow me with the boys as soon as you can."

"Will do," Sam said, and then added. "You be careful. You know what they say about a wounded animal."

Tye nodded, tipped his hat to the young lady and reined Sandy around and headed west after a man he figured would be a hell of a lot more dangerous than any wounded animal.

Chapter Twenty Two

Two Bears walked his pony along a dry wash's sandy bottom. He had ran the horse till he was ready to flounder before slowing down to a trot then a walk. He found a little pocket of rocks in the shade of the overhang of the wash which had a little water left in it from the last rain. He still had water in his canteen and didn't really want to drink the hot, stale water in the basin. His pony had no qualms about the water. As soon as his master jumped off he headed for it and started sucking up the water..

Two Bears walked to the overhang and sat down in the shade and for the first time took time to look at his wound. It wasn't much, a crease along his upper arm half way between his elbow and shoulder. It was painful, but he could live with it. He would find another homestead and get some whiskey to pour on it. It would be dark soon so he leaned his head back against the wash's wall and closed his eyes to rest for awhile..

Rest would not come as an image of that Red headed girl was fresh in his mind. *I would have had her if those bluecoats had not come along,* He thought as another image came to him. *The crazy one who charged and shot me was not wearing the blue uniform.* "A scout," he said out loud causing his pony to raise his head from the pool of water, look at him and twitch his ears. *A scout, it was a damn scout. It wasn't an accident they happen to be in the vicinity and saw my tracks. They were following me* .He smiled as a new thought came to him. *From here on out we will see just how good that scout is before I kill him.*

Sam was reluctant to leave the homestead. He was infatuated with the red headed girl and to his surprise; she was real friendly to him. Promising to come back real soon he, Wes, and the other two soldiers left, following Tye's trail. This only after advising Mr. Schaffer it might be wise to keep a gun handy in the future and don't get real friendly with any one passing by they did not know.

Tye was close to the breed; he could feel it, but the sun was dropping quickly behind the hills and following a man like the breed in the dark could get you killed. He found a place to camp just before full dark set in and waited for Sam and the others. He hoped they were close to where he was. He lit a fire, a bigger than normal fire in hopes they could find him. He was on the east side of a hill and the breed was west of him, so Tye didn't figure he would not see the fire and he hoped no other unfriendly men did.

Tye heard them five minute before they came into the glow of the campfire. He was sitting on a log sipping some hot coffee when they rode in. Noticing Tye sitting there drinking coffee like he had no care in the world Sam said.

"You'd been in a hell of a fix is it wasn't us coming into camp with you holding a cup of coffee instead of a gun."

"Wasn't a doubt in my mind that it wasn't you," Tye offered with a smile.

"And how's that?"

'Only people I know that makes as much racket as ya'll was making is the U.S.Calvary."

Wes cut loose with a howl of laughter. "That's sho'nuf tha truth Mr. Tye." The others were laughing as they dismounted and picketed their horses. Each man brought his tin and filled it with the coffee. Tye pulled some of the big sticks out of the fire and put sand on them to make the fire smaller.

"How's Cranston doing?"

"He's gonna be fine," Wes said. "That Mrs. Schaffer, now she is one fine lady and a first class doctor."

Didn't think we wus gonna ever leave that place cause ole' Sam here was all google eyed over that daughter of hers," James said laughing.

"Is that a fact?" Tye said smiling and looking at Sam who was obliviously embarrassed by the talk.

"Well...she's a mighty fine lady. She can cook, keep house, saddle and ride a horse, knows how to shoot..."

"Whoa there boy." Tye said laughing and giving a wink to the soldiers. "You don't have to justify to me or these men as to why you are all slobbered face over a woman.'"

"I'm not all slob..." he said emphatically then stopped and laughed when he saw they were all joshing him. "Well, anyway she a fine young lady and I intend to see her again. So that's the end of it."

Wes asked. "How close are we to the breed?"

"Close enough that I didn't want to stumble into him in the dark trying to track him." He took a sip of coffee and then said. "About midnight I am going to take a stroll on foot and see if I can sniff out his camp."

"By yourself?" Wes asked.

Tye nodded, "Unless any of you boys have these," he said pointing to his Apache knee high moccasins. A man can move might quiet in these compared to the leather soled boots you are wearing."

"I understand that, but still, all alone?" Sam stated.

"I learned a long time ago that when I was on scout it was a lot easier by yourself because you know you own abilities and you don't have to worry about someone else and you can concentrate on the task at hand a lot better. That's no reflection on any of yawls' abilities, just the way it is." He poured himself another cup. "Just about enough for one more cup for everyone." He topped off each man's cup.

"Anything to eat?" the trooper named Lester asked.

"I swear Lester, that's all you think about is your stomach," James said. Everyone laughed.

"In the pack over there," James said nodding toward where the saddles were, "Are some sourdough biscuits and bacon. Grab a skillet and we can warm them up and have a soldiers feast." Once again everyone had a good chuckle.

"My moma tol me one time," Lester said. "Boy, don't you ever take on a job with a empty belly." He laughed and added. 'I figure with this here job, I got a good chance of dying and I sure don't want to meet my Maker with an empty, growling belly," drawing more laughs.

This is as good of bunch of men as I have ever been with, Tye thought to himself. Every one of them would look the devil in the eye and spit on him. He smiled remembering what his pa had said about men like these. *"They would do to ride the river with."* He looked over at Sam drinking his coffee and asked.

"Just how old are you Sam?"

"Twenty four by my date of birth," he said then added. "My body sometimes tells me I'm pushing sixty."

Tye and the others laughed. "Why's that Sam?" Wes asked.

"Till I became a deputy I busted horses and I'm telling you the truth when I say that's not a career I would recommend to anyone," then added. "Except a man I didn't like."

"Tye," Wes said, "We and tha uthers bac at tha fort been heering fur a long time 'bout you. Tha stories true?"

"Reckon it depends on what you heard," Tye answered. "Been out here all my life. I was born and raised on a small piece of land about forty five miles southwest of Fort Clark near the border." Tye paused long enough to swallow the last of his coffee. He didn't like talking about himself, but he liked these men and they were asking and since it was still too early to bed down he talked. He told them about his ma and pa and how his pa had taught him everything he knew about fighting, trapping, tracking, and living off the land. Told him about the Apache he had killed with a knife when he was fourteen and about his time with the rangers when his pa was killed. He briefly told them about his scouting at Clark and some of the men he had tracked down and killed or brought in. "That's about it," he finally said. "Got ,married to the prettiest lady in Texas and we now have two youngsters."

"You left out the best parts," Sam said chuckling.

Tye looked at him. "And what might that be?"

"Oh, just a few small details such as the tracking down the Apache Tanza all by yourself, killing him and bringing in seven small children he had captured. Or how about Grey Owl and perhaps the best Apache fighter of them all-Ke-ah. Oh yeah, I forgot to mention Yancey Cates and his band of cut-throats and then there was Alex

Vasquez and his gang." He looked at Tye. "Did I forget anyone?"

Tye laughed. "You're the one talking."

Sam looked at the soldiers. He's only been a marshal for three or so weeks and already has captured the Frazier gang that had robbed and killed no telling how many innocent folks and just three days ago tracked down and killed a vicious killer by the name of Jack Gillespie, better known as Bloody Jack. Oh yeah," he added. "He's saved every damn soldiers butt at the fort at least once and even a troop from Fort Inge led by a young lieutenant…What was his name Tye?"

"Rogers".

"Yeah, a Lieutenant Rogers and these are just some of the stories I heard about no telling how many I didn't."

"Them true Mr. Tye?" Wes asked.

Tye nodded and said. "Yes" He looked at Sam and added. "Course like all stories they sometimes get bent out of proportion by the men telling them over time."

"Such as?" Sam questioned.

"The tale of me tracking down Tanza and six of his warriors and killing them all in hand to hand fighting."

"That part of Mr. Sam"s story not true? The private named James asked.

"Most of it, but there was only two, not six warriors with Tanza." Tye chuckled, then added, "And there was only four children not seven."

"I stand corrected," Sam said laughing. "You killed three instead of six with a knife. How about the big fight recently with Yahzie and three hundred warriors that had you and a patrol pinned down."

Tye shook his head. "There wasn't three hundred only about seventy or eighty."

"What about at the end of the battle when the soldier I was talking to, who was there by the way, when all was lost and the soldiers were being overrun you started screaming like an Apache and ran thru the wallow where ya'll had been fighting from swinging an Sharps rifle like an axe and smiting down the heathens like Sampson slayed the Philistines in the Bible with the jaw of an ass. You deny that Mr. Watkins?"

Tye shook his head. "That part was true. Still don't know what prompted me to do that."

"Well whatever the reason the soldier told me it scared the hell out of the Apaches and they high tailed it out of there away from that crazy white man."

Tye, tired of the talk being about him stood up. "Ya'll can go ahead and talk. But I'm going to check the horses and make a round of the camp to make sure all is okay and then turn in. Ya'll work out a schedule for sentry duty. I'll take the last watch." He walked toward the horse and every man's eye followed him to where the horses were picketed.

"You think all them stories about him are true, Mr. Sam," James asked?

"Not a doubt in my mind," Sam replied. "That last fight he had before he became a marshal was typical Tye according to the soldier I was talking to who was in that ditch and was wounded by one of Yahzie's warriors. Not only did he end the fight with that charge yelling and swinging the Sharps, but the night before he had crawled out of the ditch and found the Apache who had been pinning them down with a 'big fifty' buffalo gun. Crawled right through all them Injuns, found the one with the gun, knifed him and brought the gun back. Then there was one of his scouts, Dan August, who I spend several hours with while he was taking me to meet Tye who told me stories that was hard to believe, but he swore were true." He drained the last of his coffee and stood up. "Yup, there's not a doubt in my mind they are true. Hell,you boys seen him charge that breed today when we was trapped like fish in a barrel. Make up your own mind. For me I'm taking the first watch and ya'll work out the rest of the schedule." He picked up his rifle and walked outside the camp.

Wes made out the order of the sentry duty. James would take the watch after Sam, then Lester, and he would take the one before Tye. They were all bedded down before Tye came back and laid down on his bedroll. As was his custom he only took off his hat and boots and laid his gun belt within easy reach. He stuck the big Bowie in the ground beside him and fell quickly asleep with his hand on the handle.

Before midnight and as James replaced Sam on guard duty, the breed watched the camp from only a few feet away. He had doubled back to get a closer look at the men trailing him and specifically the scout. He had been close enough to hear them talking, not every word said, but enough to hear the one word he wanted to hear-the scout's name. When he heard the name Watkins a shiver went down his spine. He had never seen the man, but every man on the run in the State of Texas he suspected had heard of him. He watched him taking care of the horses and decided he would shoot him and run like hell. The others he figured wouldn't be able to track him.

He shifted slightly so he could raise his Henry and shoot the damn scout. Now was perfect as Watkins had his back to him and he had no qualms about shooting a man in the back if he had to. He hesitated because Tye moved and a horse was now between him and the man he wanted to shoot. He lowered the gun and watched Tye curry the big horse which was the most magnificent animal Two Bears had ever saw. As he watched Tye came back around the horse and again had his back to him. It was dark but at this close range he figured he could hit the scout. Hell, he was one the biggest men he had ever seen. *Too big a target to miss at this range even in the poor light,* he thought.

He was raising his rifle again when he saw Tye stiffen then drop to one knee and pull his Colt. He was looking right at where Two Bears sat. Two Bears froze.

How did he know I was here, he wondered. *He must be truly a fighting man like I heard and he just felt danger for I made no sound.* He held his breath as Tye looked his way. He could feel the man's eyes on him but he knew he could not see him-at least no normal man could. *But this is no normal man,* he thought to himself. As he watched, another man came and sat down with his back to a large rock and laid his rifle across his lap.

"Better get some sleep, Tye. I'm taking the first watch," Sam said.

Tye stood up and holstered his gun. Which Sam had not noticed was in his hand.

"Hear something?"

Tye walked by where Sam sat and squatted beside him. "No, but I had a sudden feeling something, or someone, was out there. I didn't see anything, but you stay alert Sam. Don't forget this man we're after is half Indian and he can slit your throat before you even know he's around, so be careful and you tell the man who replaces you the same."

"Will do Tye." He watched as Tye made his way to his bedroll. Sam began to listen to the sounds of the night. his senses getting accustom to them: a cricket; a owl's wings as the big bird flew overhead looking for a meal; some small animal, probably a pack rat or rabbit scurrying away to hide from the owl's eyes; the fast beat of the wings of bats searching the night sky for insects; and in the distance a coyote began his mournful howling as the moon made an appearance. Any unusual sound would alert him to trouble. He was wide awake and would remain so. Two Bears noticed this and decided he would wait before making his way away from the camp. It was too risky to try anything now.

Two Bears, who had dozed off himself, was suddenly awakened by voices. He silently cursed himself for dozing, but now, wide awake and alert, he listened. A changing of the guards was taking place and he knew he would kill at least one bluecoat because as he watched the new one was stretching and yawning, not nearly alert as the man in plain clothes was. He knew that the man would doze off so he waited. Thirty minutes later he made his move.

Moving carefully and silently in his moccasins he moved behind the man and then waited, listening. Steady breathing told him the man was asleep. He slipped his butcher knife from its sheath and moved within a step of where the soldier sat, his rifle lying across his thighs, his chin on his chest-asleep.

Chapter Twenty Three

James's eyes flew open when a hand clamped over his moth and jerked his head back. He only got a glimpse of the blade before it was imbedded deep in his chest. He struggled for a few seconds as blood poured from his mouth and ran between Two Bears fingers. The soldier's body stiffened as he took a deep breath and then relaxed as the last bit of life drained from him.

Two Bears stood over the soldier and knocked the cap from the dead man's head intending to scalp him. He cursed when he saw the short hair of the soldier and pushed the soldier on his side. He jerked around and had his pistol in his hand when he heard a voice and boots scraping on the rocks that covered the area. He didn't hesitate and silently went into the brush headed for his horse.

"James...James you okay?" The man asked. The man coming was Wes and he dropped to one knee and leveled his rifle when he saw James lying on the ground.

"Tye," he shouted. "Tye, over here, quick."

Five seconds later, Tye, Sam, and Lester were there.

"Damn," Tye cursed. "Damn it all to hell," he said as he rushed over to where the soldier lay. He knew immediately he was dead and looked quickly around just as they all heard the pounding of a horse's hooves on the rocky ground. Tye shoved his Colt under his belt on his pants since his holster and gun belt was beside his bedroll. He knelt by James and rolled him gently onto his back. The dead soldier's eyes were still open. Placing his hand over James's eyes, Tye closed them and stood up. Tears flowed down both Wes's and Lester's cheeks as they openly wept at their friends death.

"Sam," Tye said, "Take Wes and Lester back to camp. I'll do what's necessary here."

Wes spoke up. "If'n yu don't mind suh, Lester and me would like ta take care of James. We kno'd him a long time suh and we would like to see him to his final resting place." Tye put his hand on the soldier's shoulder and nodded. He and Sam made their way back to camp.

"My fault, Dammit,"Sam said. "My fault," he repeated and slammed his fist on his leg.

"Why is it your fault?" Tye asked.

"I knew he was sleepy. He was yawning when I left him."

"Did you tell him what I said?"

Sam nodded. "I told him, but I could tell he wasn't wide awake."

"He was a soldier Sam. Every minute of every day you are in the field could be every soldier's last. They know it and accept it. You did what you had to do and told him to stay alert."

"I know that, but still I…" his voice trailed off to a whisper that Tye could not hear. Tye knew the feeling as he had lost friends when he shouldn't have. His mind went back to the Turley's who help raise him, to his good friends, Lieutenant Garrison and Sergeant Christian, and others who had been killed over the years. It was a feeling of, I might have done more, or I should have been there and things might have been different. A lump came to his throat when he thought of his pa dying in his arms and his mother slowly dying of a broken heart. He shook these thoughts off and turned to Sam.

"Sam. When the others get here ya'll follow me. I'm going after that bastard while the trail is hot." That said. He tightened the girth on his saddle and then mounting Sandy, headed west.

"Be careful, Tye." Sam hollered. "That son-of-a-bitch is liable to ambush you as not."

The trail was plain and Tye followed on Sandy at a canter. He kept one eye on the tracks, one on likely ambush spots, and both on Sandy's ears at times. A good horse can sure help a fellow if he pays attention and Sandy's spotting trouble and warning him with a twitch of his ears or a snort and shake of his heard had saved him on more than one occasion.

After an hour on the trail Tye pulled up, took his canteen that was strapped around his saddle horn and took a small amount in his mouth, swished it around and spit it out. After taking drink, he stepped down from the saddle and poured a little in his hat to let Sandy suck it up. He was looking at the hills ahead of him while Sandy drank when he saw a flash of light. Years of tracking and fighting experience under his belt told him to pretend he didn't see it so whoever was there didn't know he had been spotted. He marked the spot in his mind and went about pretending to be occupied messing with his saddle bags and saddle while watching the spot without being obvious. He wasn't worried about being shot because the reflection was over a half mile away. He figured it was the breed waiting on him to get close enough for a killing shot. Very few things he knew of that weren't man made reflected sun light and he was sure it came from the barrel of a rifle or maybe the breed was dumb enough to wear something that would reflect sunlight. He already figured the breed has not being stupid so he figured it was a rifle. He mounted Sandy and walked him toward the jumble of rocks and clumps of cedars and cactus where he had seen the flash come from.

The breed smiled. *Maybe the great Watkins is not as smart as I have heard,* he thought as he watched the man getting closer and closer. He had his rifle sighted on the chest of the big man. As he watched, the horse and rider disappeared behind a huge boulder that was as big as a house. He swung the barrel of his Henry slightly to the left aiming at the spot where horse and rider would appear on this side of the boulder. When the horses head showed he began squeezing the trigger. The breed smiled. There was no way he could miss at this range.

Chapter Twenty Four

The breed's eyes widen. "What the hell?" he mumbled. There was no rider on the horse. He quickly looked at the other side of the boulder where horse and rider had disappeared a moment before. Nothing moved. He could see the horse walking, heading on up the trail but not hide nor hair of its rider. Sweat broke out on the breed's forehead and trickled down his face and across his eyebrows and into his eyes making them burn. He blinked and quickly wiped his eyes to get the stinging drops of salt out of them. He looked to the left and right toward the rocks below him and saw nothing. For the first time that he could remember he felt a twinge of fear. He had always been in control of situations like this with him being the hunter-now he knew he was the hunted and it scared the hell out of him. He was battle-tested enough though to know that in a game of cat and mouse like this, the one who moved first was likely to die. He sat there, eyes and ears straining for the slightest movement or sound. Suddenly, it came to him and he cursed. "Damn. The son-of-a-bitch is walking beside his horse." He stood up and moved to his left following the horse but staying behind rocks when he could.

When Tye and Sandy had walked behind the huge boulder Tye dismounted and removed his Henry from its leather. He crouched on the right side of Sandy which was the side away from where the breed or whoever it was that was on the side of the rocky hill. He was elated when they emerged on the opposite side of the boulder when he saw the thick cedars and cactus that was on the upper slope side of the trail. He didn't figure the shooter could see below the saddle on Sandy's back making it easy for him to stay out of sight as he moved in a crouch beside his horse. The trail went around the side of the hill and when Tye figured they had gone far enough that the shooter could no longer see them he stopped Sandy and loosely tied him to a cedar. He started to make his way up the steep slope when he felt the air split beside his ear followed by crack of a rifle. He dropped back down to the trail and ran back where he come from staying below the tops of the cedars.

Breathing hard from the exertion of running thirty yards and from the fact he had come close to having his head blown off, he paused to think. *The breed is smart. It didn't take him long to figure out what I'd done and he just followed Sandy till I showed myself. Now, I don't know where the hell he is.* Another thought came to him, one that might be in his favor. *He may be thinking he hit me and might just show himself.* He moved back the way he had come until he could see Sandy. He crouched, leaning his Henry against a cedar and pulled his Colt. Any shooting now would be close quarters and he was more comfortable with his single action Colt in close quarters. He pulled the hammer back and waited.

Five agonizing minutes went by with no sound-ten minutes and just when Tye was thinking the shooter had lit a shuck he heard Sandy whinny. "The bastard is behind me and trying to steal Sandy," he mumbled as he stood and ran back down the trail toward Sandy. Hooves pounding rocks more whinnying and snorting, and a man cursing convinced him he was right.

As he rounded the bend in the trail he saw a man lying on his back and pointing his gun at Sandy. Tye fired from the hip and his bullet clipped a rock next to the man's head. The breed, or who Ty figured was the breed, fired a quick shot at Tye and then rolled into the cedars out of sight. The slug whistled by Tye's head.

"Here Sandy" Tye hollered and then again, "Here." He wanted the big horses away from the breed and out of danger. He figured Sandy had knocked the man down and was fixing to stomp him after tearing the reins loose from the cedar branch. Tye fired three more quick shots into the cedars where the man had gone as Sandy came to him. Tye patted his friend on the neck as Sandy rubbed his nose on Tye's shoulder. The only sound was Tye's and Sandy's breathing as he stood there, ears tuned for any sound.

"That damn scout is good," Two Bears mumbled, cursing as he ran for his horse. He jumped into the saddle and kicked his horse into a gallop. He looked over his shoulder as he topped a hill and saw a puff of smoke from the scouts rifle. An instant later his hat was blown off his head.

Cursing, the breed laid low in the saddle as another round split the air above him. "I'm gonna kill that sumbitching bastard,' he mumbled. An instant later he was over the hill and out of sight.

Tye, when he first heard the horse running, holstered his Colt and picked up his Henry that he had left earlier and fired when saw the man top the hill. He saw the man's hat fly off and fired again before he disappeared. Three seconds later he was on Sandy and in pursuit of the man called Two Bears.

Two hundred yards down the trail, Sam and the soldiers appeared and the seen Tye and Sandy topping a hill off to their right. They had been coming in a hurry since they had heard the shots and they veered off the trail and nudged their horses to a faster pace following Tye. With the rocks, cedars and huge clumps of cactus everywhere, it was impossible for the horses to run all out. They only caught glimpses of Tye every few seconds as he was getting farther away from them. *That damn horse of his must be part mountain goat,* Sam thought as his horse righted himself after stumbling and almost going down.

Tye reined in Sandy and sat listening. He heard no hoof beats, no sound of any kind. He quickly dismounted as he knew the breed had and was waiting to ambush him again. Dropping the reins he scurried into the brush to think what to do. He knew that the man was no more than a hundred or so yards away because he had caught a glimpse of him a moment before reining in Sandy. A few minutes ago he was hidden waiting on the breed to make a mistake and show himself. Now the roles were reversed. He was going to have to flush him out and that was going to take some work-and luck.

He started to move when he heard the sound of hooves striking rocks and he knew it was Sam. He also knew the men were riding into a death trap. He hollered.

"Get off your horses and get down." An instant later he heard the crack of a rifle and Sam tumbled off his horse hitting the ground hard. His startled horse ran off. Wes and Lester were on the ground and scrambled to the fallen deputy.

"How is he?" Tye asked.

"Hit in the shoulder," Wes answered, he'll live.

"Drag him into the brush and you two stay with him. I'm gonna flush him out. Keep those rifles cocked and ready."

"Yes Suh Mr. Tye." Wes said. "You be damn careful, you hear."

Tye didn't answer as he had already moved a few feet and didn't want to give his new position away. Sweat ran freely down his face and on down his collar.

Two Bears was sweating profusely. He wanted to shoot Watkins but could not feel too bad since the shot hit the other white man. He was confident that he could kill all of them. He would take them as the opportunity came no matter which one it was. The man he shot would be dead if the shout from Tye as he was squeezing the trigger had not caused the man to shift his position at the exact time the Henry belched its deadly slug. With one down and three left he would head out again and set up another ambush and then another till they were all dead. He winced as he stood up to leave. The wounds from those damn Watkins bullets had quit bleeding, but pained him when he moved. They were only flesh wounds, but he would have to find a doctor when he got to Mexico. In the mean time he hoped the rot gut he poured on them would keep the infection down. If it didn't it would be a hell of a waste of good sipping whiskey.

He took one step toward where he had left his mount when his hat flew off his head an instant before the crack of a rifle reached his ears. He hit the ground hard and rolled behind a cedar and quickly searched the area where he figured the shot had come from. He saw nothing. As he desperately tried to find the shooter he heard a voice shouting at him.

"Give it up kid. I could have drilled you square if I had wanted to."

He knew the voice had to be that of the scout Watkins. "Forget that horseshit Watkins. If you want me you'll have to come and get me." He chambered a shell in his Henry and waited.

A half hour passed and the kid had still seen no movement or heard any sound. He was part Injun and Injuns was known for their patience, but the white man part of him had none. He shifted his position slightly so he could easily get his feet under him so he could make break for it. As he did he felt the whisper as a slug cut the air by his ear. He dropped back down cursing.

"That's twice I could have drilled you kid. The next time I will," Tye shouted.

The kid looked around and cursed. The spot he had taken to ambush the men only had one way out and that was blocked by Watkins. He rolled on his back to look behind him and then had to try and wiggle his body deeper into the ground as another bullet clipped a branch off the cedar only inches from his face. He knew he was in a hopeless situation here and he weighed his chances of jumping up and running as fast as he could toward where his horse was tied and getting the hell out of here. He figured the odds were low that he could make it. He'd already seen just how good a shot Watkins was. *It's a long way to any town where they would have to take me,* he thought, *and a lot can happen between now and then.*

"All right," he shouted. "Here's my rifle," he said tossing it out from where he lay.

"Toss you pistol out too," Tye shouted back. "And stand up slowly with your hands so I can see them." The kid did as he was told. As soon as he stood up Tye appeared from behind a boulder that was partially concealed by two thick cedars only forty yards from where the kid had lay.

"Get your hands over your head and don't' even blink or I'll gut shoot you," Tye said as he moved slowly and cautiously toward his quarry. The muzzle of the Henry never moved from the kid's chest. Two Bears knew he was only a twitch of Tye's finger from instant death or in the case of a stomach shot, a long and painful one.

"Wes," Tye shouted. "You and Lester get up here with some rope."

While they waited Two Bears asked. "I've heard of you Watkins. Hard you were a man who could walk on water and the army down at Clark would be lost without you. Heard not even the Apaches could kill you. What the hell you doing scouting way up here?"

"Ain't scouting no more kid."

"You ain't scouting. Then why you way up here?"

"Got a new job."

"Yeah. And what's that?"

"Tracking down vermin like you. I'm a Deputy U.S. Marshal now."

"The kid swore loudly. "You...a son-of-a-bitching lawdog?"

"Yep,'Tye replied. "A law dog that's taking you back to a likley hanging."

As Wes and Lester came on the scene they heard the outlaw shout. "I ain't gonna hang you bastard. It's a long way back to Stockton or wherever you are taking me."

"Tye him tight, after you find that knife that's on him," Tye said as the two soldiers stood by his side. "Hanging or shot, kid. Either way you are dead. You've killed a lot of innocent people and you're gonna have to pay for it. Now lie on the ground and put your hands behind your back," he said after Wes tossed the knife to Lester who handed it to Tye before crouching down beside the outlaw.

Lester jerked the man's hands up higher on his back and Two Bears winched as pain shot up his shoulder from one of the wounds inflicted by Tye.

"That hurt sum," Lester said. "Wal, you hurt the hell out my Lootenant." He jerked again and another moan came from Two Bears. Lester stood up and kicked the prone man in the ribs. "That's for my friend James you killed."

"That's enough Lester," Tye said.

"I'll kill you for that," Two Bears hissed through clinched teeth. "You're a dead man you black bastard." Lester drew his boot back for another kick but Tye"s voice stopped him.

"I said that's enough. The law will take care of him. He'll pay for what he's done."

"A hanging is too quick for this here scum, suh."

Tye placed his hand on the soldiers shoulder. "It ain't the hanging that's bad, Lester. It's the wait knowing you are going to die on a certain day that's tough on a man."

Lester looked at Tye, smiled and nodded. "Yur right suh. I never tho'ght abut it that way." He laughed. 'No suh, never tho'ght abut it that way.

Every second of the trip Two Bears was looking for a chance to make a break, but Watkins was always a step ahead of him. When he had to answer natures call at least two rifles was on him. They did not untie his hands so he could eat and was fed by one of the men with another sitting nearby with a rifle. Bed time found him hog tied like a pig on a spit over a fire. He knew the way all of them felt about him and would not hesitate for a second to kill him

."Get him on his feet and let's get to Fort Stockton," Tye said the as they broke their last camp. The fort and the guardhouse were about four hours away.

On the way back they had stopped and picked up the wounded Cranston and had Sam's shoulder looked after by Mrs. Schaffer. They delivered Jamie Kindle, alias Two Bears, to an elated Major Harwell. A couple hours later, after Sam received some more medical attention, the two men were on their way back to Fort Clark.

Sam looked over at Tye and chuckled. "You know partner, riding with you can be dangerous to a man's health."

Tye thought about his dead friends and his pa for a moment. "That's the damn truth Sam if you think about it," Then added. "You want another partner?"

Gary McMillan

"Hell no, Tye. Why would I want to have another partner that would probably only get the easy jobs like serving warrants or arresting drunks when I can ride with you and get shot at every damn day and twice on Sunday." Both men laughed and Tye knew he had more than just a partner; he had a friend that he could depend on when things got tough and if need be, probably risk his life to save him just like he would for him.

"No," Tye replied. "Why would a man give up a easy, boring job when he can have fun like we are having."

Sam, pointing to his shoulder laughed. "And have a good chance of receiving one of these." Tye reached over and slapped him on his good shoulder.

"Lets get to Clark," he said then added, "Partner." They kicked their mounts into an easy gallop toward home.

287

Epilogue

A week after Tye had gotten back home word came that the Frazier brothers had been hung in San Antonio in front of the largest crowd ever to witness a hanging in the state of Texas. A couple days later a dispatch came from Fort Stockton that Kindle (Two Bears) had been bayoneted to death while trying to escape from his cell. Tye wondered if Lester was the one who did the honors. He smiled at the thought.

Everything was great here at Fort Clark. Dan was doing a great job as chief of scouts according to Major Thurston. The babies were growing every day and Rebecca was as lovely as ever. Buff was spoiling the babies rotten and was happier than Tye had ever seen the old mountain man.

Tye was sitting on his porch studying the list of wanted men trying to decide who he would go after next when Sam walked up.

"How's the shoulder Sam?"

Sam lifted his arm to shoulder height and rotated it. "Fit as a fiddle."

Tye smiled as he saw his friend wince just a little. Sam, noticing the list of names Tye was looking at said. "You can put that list away. We got orders." Sam Chuckled. "I don't know if being hooked with you is such a good deal for me."

"Why do you say that?"

"With your reputation we are getting all the 'shit jobs'.

"Shit jobs?" Tye questioned.

"Yeah, you know the tough ones no one else could do." He handed the paper with the orders to Tye which Tye read and then whistled.

"I see what you mean." Tye said as Sam sat down beside him on the steps. Tye read the paper again.

An outlaw gang led by two brothers, Willie and Lester Mills, are headed your way. They left San Antonio after holding up the Buckhorn Saloon and its patrons. They took four thousand dollars from the saloons safe and an unknown amount from several customers that were there. They killed three of the customers who refused to give them their money and killed two more citizens as they rode out of town.

The brothers are known killers who have eluded capture for over two years. They are vicious men who kill when there is no reason so be on the lookout for them. There are six in the gang beside the brothers.

"Welcome to your new job, Tye." Sam laughed.

"From what I've seen so far it doesn't get any easier." He stood up. "Do you think we need to get to Uvalde since it's located between here and San Antonio to see if they have showed up there?"

"That's my thinking," Sam answered.

"Give me an hour to get things together," then added. "In the meantime while I'm getting ready why don't you go to town and pick us up some supplies for a week at the mercantile store." He handed five dollars to Sam. "This ought to pay for my half." Sam nodded and left. Tye took a deep breath and headed back into the house to tell Rebecca and get his things together. Leaving was the toughest thing about this job.

Read book ten of the Tye Watkins series:

A Reason to Kill

Tye Watkins-U.S. Marshall

www.ingramcontent.com/pod-product-compliance
Lightning Source LLC
Chambersburg PA
CBHW021334250626
47155CB00002B/695